www.ingramcontent.com/pod-product-compliance
Lightning Source LLC
Chambersburg PA
CBHW011513170626
46810CB00009B/3348

Acknowledgements

The author would like to thank:

Dr Hannah Straw, who goes about knowing actual facts while I busy myself making stuff up.

Scarlet Hall and Hero Hall, who have long tolerated (while secretly enjoying) deep-dive revisitations of, to their upsettingly young minds, thoroughly ancient television programmes and pretended to believe me when I said it was for work.

Barnaby Eaton-Jones who has, on multiple occasions, trusted me to muck about in universes near to my heart. He is my TIM, albeit more hirsute.

Bryan Stanion, Professor Cawston himself, who once directed me in a play and was charmingly tolerant of the fannish gleam in my eye.

Everyone involved in The Tomorrow People television series, books and audio dramas past for their storytelling prowess and those involved with the current novel series for their forbearance in accepting a Canadian interloper into the fold. Especially Paul Simpson, editor extraordinaire.

And, of course, Roger Price, Brian Finch and co. for bringing the Tomorrow People to life in the first place.

From the Author

I was a peculiar child, a statement that will occasion little surprise amongst those who have met any author and none at all in those have encountered this one.

Growing up in Canada, to English parents, I often found the television dial tuned to the local PBS station and the transmissions from the motherland that seemed to make up the lion's share of its offerings. As a result, over the years, I took to my Anglophile bosom, with fervour, everything from *The Fall and Rise of Reginald Perrin* and *The Good Life* to *All Creatures Great & Small* and *The Adventures of Sherlock Holmes*.

Science fiction, however, was my first love and there were soon a number of British series that had become required viewing. A certain long-standing traveller in time and space set up camp forever in

my soul, as did the denizens of the mining ship *Red Dwarf*, those who knew where their towels were and the rebels that fought alongside and occasionally against Roj Blake.

I don't recall precisely when *The Tomorrow People* joined the pantheon. I was three when the original series ended, toddling around the aforementioned maple-based country, and thus missed its original ITV broadcasts on multiple fronts. I have a sneaking suspicion that I initially sought it out on discovering Peter Davison's appearance in Series 3. I am, after all, what kinder hearted people call a *completist*. Thankfully, my obsessive nature demanded that I start at the beginning, which given the reputation of *A Man for Emily*, is probably for the best.

The important thing is that I was swiftly hooked by its premise and, by extension, the idea that, at any moment, I too might break out and take my place amongst the occupants of the Lab.

I am, many years later, still waiting for my powers to develop, but I haven't given up hope. Surely there is room for a more mature Tomorrow Person about the place, if only to file tax returns and advise on pension plans.

In the meantime, I'm delighted to accept the honour of telling a new tale about those marvellous

members of *homo superior* and their quest to save Humankind from its own worst impulses.

We need them now, more than ever.

The Tomorrow People

If you've never met the Tomorrow People before… their names are John Dixon, Stephen Jameson, Carol MacNeil and Kenny Green. Perfectly ordinary names for what might initially seem to be perfectly ordinary young people.

But spend any time in their company, and you will soon discover that they are far from ordinary. They are, in fact, the first of a new race. *Homo superior* to some. To others, *homo novus.* To themselves and anyone else with a whisper of imagination, they are The Tomorrow People. In any case, a wiser, broader-minded and infinitely more peaceful species than *homo sapiens.* Indeed, they lack their predecessors' greatest weakness: the ability to kill.

In its place, remarkable powers: Telepathy – the ability to speak to each other via thought waves. Telekinesis – the ability to move and influence

objects using only their minds. And, of course, Teleportation – the ability to think themselves from one place to another.

They call the latter 'jaunting'.

Jaunting is usually aided by specially constructed jaunting belts, designed to enable more complicated trips and prevent accidents, although short jaunts, when they can picture their destination clearly in their minds, are sometimes possible.

For the moment, as they wait eagerly for others to evolve and 'break out', they are a team of four who bear, with grace and fortitude, intergalactic responsibility for the future of planet Earth. They are guided in this by the Galactic Federation, based aboard a space station known as the Trig, who have, in addition, gifted the Tomorrow People a biotronic living computer called TIM, on the understandable grounds that 'Technobiologically Informed Mentor' is a bit of a mouthful.

They themselves, when not leading their everyday lives, work from a secret laboratory, built by John, beneath a disused London Underground Station. In truth, they spend a lot of their time there, as any young person in possession of a secret Lab might.

Their true nature is kept secret whenever possible, aware as they are that not all of mankind

would treat their existence with tolerance or under-standing.

But that doesn't mean that they are without friends in the human world. Ginge and Lefty, for instance, who, while initially in the thrall of the evil, shape-shifting robot Jedikiah, soon turned against him and became staunch allies of the Tomorrow People.

After all, in an uncertain and ever-changing world, they'll take all the help they can get.

With thanks to Roger Price and Brian Finch

THE
TOMORROW PEOPLE
PRIME FACTORS

Episode One

The sound had caught Carol entirely by surprise, worming its way into the back of her mind during some moment of distraction, with such stealth that she almost didn't hear it at all. If it hadn't grown so insistent, so clearly directed *at* her, she might have learned to tune it out entirely, long before she recognised it for the message it clearly was.

It had begun, several days previously, as an intermittent, distant thump, the kind that made you immediately want to compare notes with passers-by, to ensure your imagination wasn't playing tricks on you.

The latter idea wasn't out of the question. She was eager, as they all were, for others to break out, to reveal themselves as Tomorrow People and come into their new powers. Something that they'd quite recently been led to believe that every child had

the potential to do. Which, though an exciting prospect, had not yet come to fruition. It would be understandable if, on occasion, their desire to see their numbers expanded led them down a blind alley or two.

At first, she kept quiet about what she was experiencing, lest she excite or worry the others without cause (if anyone else had picked up the flickering signal, they too were keeping their own counsel).

Instead, she had relaxed her mind and tried to bring it into focus. It was a challenging task, like tuning a radio whose dial had been greased. Every time she thought she was about to zero in on the source, a wave of static washed over her and she was cast back into a sea of noise.

But it didn't stop her from trying.

She remembered how exciting it had been, not so long ago, when they had finally sensed Stephen's thoughts in their minds. As disorganised and loud as they had been (a cacophonous racket, frankly), their appearance had felt immediately *right*. It wasn't that they had been so desperately lonely – herself, John and Kenny – but there was, undeniably, a faint sense of incompleteness that came from knowing that there *were* others out there, destined to join

2

their ranks, and that they could do nothing but wait patiently for them to make themselves known. And, in turn, for their greatest work – leading Planet Earth towards a better future – to truly begin.

This time was different, though she could not yet articulate why, even to herself. It might even have been frightening, if not for the electric charge of curiosity that overwhelmed her doubts.

And yet answers remained frustratingly out of reach.

Until now.

Moments ago, she had heard it again and when she had stretched her mind out, expecting further vexation, it had neither resisted nor retreated, instead growing louder, deeper and more distinct.

And were those words? Actual words?

Carol felt her heart quicken as she strained to make them out. Would it be a name? A call for help? An evolving being desperate to understand what was happening to them?

She felt a sudden chill as a single phrase detached itself from the maelstrom and tumbled towards her at speed.

And then she woke, screaming.

'John!' she cried out, as she sat bolt upright from what she only realised later was a prone position on the floor of the Lab.

'Carol, thank goodness,' said John, in his even, almost patrician, tone. John Dixon was 17 years old but often seemed much older. The price, Carol assumed, of leadership. He had been the first Tomorrow Person to break out, that they knew of, and the weight of that responsibility was something he took very seriously. At times, perhaps, he took himself a little too seriously, but the others trusted and relied on him without hesitation.

Carol felt his keen, inquisitive eyes on her.

'Told you she'd be fine,' said Kenny, quickly slipping one hand behind his back, to hide the thumbnail at which he'd been unconsciously nibbling. Kenny Green was only 12 years old and usually hid behind an air of quiet mischief. Having broken out much earlier in his life than the others, his reserved cool might also have looked like the behaviour of a much older child, but it only ever reminded Carol how young he actually was. His occasional recklessness only reinforced the effect.

'I believe your actual words,' offered a disembodied voice, 'were *I think Carol's knackered*.'

'I never…' insisted Kenny, stepping away from the wall against which he'd been leaning.

'You did,' confirmed a slight teenaged figure, from beneath a mop of untidy brown hair. He was seated at the table in the centre of the room and only just hid a half smile, half smirk, equal parts relief and amusement. Stephen Jameson was 14 and seemed 14, for better or worse.

'My memory files are seldom inaccurate,' added the unseen contributor – better known as TIM, the biotronic living computer that aided them in all of their adventures. 'I can replay the recording, if it would help.'

Kenny shook his head.

'Don't bother. I'm just glad Carol's okay.'

'Are you okay?' John asked Carol, extending a hand and helping her to her feet.

She took a moment to find her bearings, fighting off a wave of dizziness and uncertainty.

I am Carol MacNeil, she told herself firmly. I am 16 years old, and I have a job to do.

'I think so. What happened?'

'You have been unconscious for several hours.' TIM made the revelation without drama, as always.

'Hours!' she exclaimed. That couldn't be possible. It felt as if minutes had passed, at most. She'd been sitting at the table in the Lab, she remembered that much. Staring idly at the shifting patterns of light on the ceiling and the dangling lengths of tubing, listening intently for any sign of what she had come to believe, or certainly hope, was someone about to break out. So focused had she been on finding it, it had once again caught her off-guard.

'We tried to get through to you.' John ran a hand apologetically through his dark hair. 'Your mind wouldn't let us in.'

'We even tried to link,' added Kenny.

'But it was like something was getting in the way,' said Stephen. 'Like we were being pushed back.'

'I was unable, however,' said TIM, 'to detect any unexpected telepathic activity.' The computer's voice was neutral but nonetheless gave off the impression that the lack of available information was a personal affront.

Carol felt a pang of guilt. They must have been so worried about her. She'd have been distraught if it had happened to one of them. And more than a little upset if it had been the result of their not sharing important information.

She looked at them each in turn. Her decision to keep them in the dark felt difficult to defend now. More than that – it no longer felt like a decision she had made for herself.

'I think,' she said finally, 'that there's something I need to tell you.'

'Are you sure that's what you heard?' asked John, some minutes later, after Carol had haltingly laid out the events of the past few days. To his credit, he had kept any anger he harboured towards her secrecy at bay. His tone was firm, but there was no doubting that her well-being was his primary concern.

'I'm sure,' she said, then repeated the message with as little emotion as she could manage: 'Stop me, before I do it again.' She found herself trembling, as if the fear she ought to have felt from the beginning was catching up with her. 'But what does it mean? Do what again?'

'I don't know,' said John thoughtfully. 'But it doesn't sound good.'

'Do you really think it was one of us?' asked Kenny.

'I don't!' Stephen folded his arms across his chest, to underline his disapproval.

Carol stood up, exasperated.

'What else could it be?'

'You have to admit, Carol,' John said gently, 'it doesn't sound much like something a Tomorrow Person would say.'

'How do we know?' Beneath her blonde fringe, tears had formed in the young woman's eyes. 'How many breakouts have we actually experienced?'

The question was easily answered by counting the occupants of the room, but Carol rolled straight on.

'That's right. Four. And even then, it was slightly different for all of us. And never what you might call easy. We've no idea what this person is going through. They could be in tremendous pain and confusion.'

'Or they could be a nutter,' suggested Stephen.

'That's not a very nice word.'

Stephen blushed. Carol might only have been two years older than he was, but when she told him off, it felt uncomfortably parental.

'Maybe not,' he replied defiantly, 'but whatever it is they think they're going to do again, I don't want them to do it here.'

John broke in before the tension got out of hand.

'Carol's right,' he said. 'If this *is* someone breaking out, we obviously need to find out for sure. Besides, whoever they are, whatever they're experiencing, they are asking for help. If we don't help them, who will?'

No one seemed in much of a hurry to argue, however much Kenny and Stephen glowered.

'So, what do we do next?' asked Carol.

'We reach out again, see if we can't get a lock on our mysterious caller. Only this time...' John looked at Carol and she felt a hint of kindly reproof. '...we do it together.'

Now he looked around the group.

'Agreed?'

Without further prompting, Stephen and Kenny both nodded. If they were headed down a dangerous road, at least they'd be doing it as a team.

'Right, that's decided. Now, let's link.'

Carol returned to her seat. Then she placed her hands on the table, palms down. John did the same, his fingertips touching hers. Stephen and Kenny followed suit, until all eight hands connected.

'TIM?'

'Yes, John?'

'Ordinarily, I'd leave one of us in charge, but we're going to need everyone's power to pull this off. Can we count on you to keep an eye on things?'

'Of course, John.'

'If anything goes wrong, let Ginge and Lefty know.'

TIM paused before replying, carefully.

'Mister Harding and Mister Leftridge are trustworthy associates, but neither have telepathic abilities. I am unsure what they would be able to do. Should anything go amiss.'

'If we've learned anything by now, it's that sometimes we need a literal helping hand or two. Besides, I'd hate you to think we'd left you entirely on your own.'

It would be difficult to argue that TIM was moved by John's consideration, in the traditional sense, but the brief hesitation before he replied did suggest, at very least, a certain amount of appreciation.

'Very well. As you see fit.'

'Thank you, TIM.'

John refocused his attention on the others.

'Now, let's see who's out there.'

Like tendrils of ivy creeping steadily up a garden wall, the four minds spread out into the world. It might have felt like searching for a psychic needle in a telepathic haystack, were it not for one thing: they knew that whatever the source, it was not an ordinary mind.

After all, it could make itself heard, consciously or not, which meant it was telepathic to some degree. Whether that meant it was a newly evolving Tomorrow Person, a member of an advanced alien race or something entirely new remained to be seen.

There were other reasons to be hopeful, however unsettling the message had been. Whoever had sent it had requested help, which hopefully meant it wasn't going to actively close its mind to them. And likely wouldn't resist their efforts on its behalf.

The only real concern was whether they were already too late and whatever it was feared would happen again had already done so.

In which case, the best-case scenario was that they had found a new Tomorrow Person. The Prime Barrier – the biological inability to kill they all possessed – would certainly be a very useful preventative to have in their corner. At least no lives would be lost.

'Oh my!' said Carol, though not aloud. She was

communicating with the others telepathically now, her voice in their heads. It was one of the gifts of their kind and meant that they were never alone unless they wished to be. It was usually a great comfort.

Now, however, there was a hint of pain in her interior voice.

'Yes,' replied John. 'I feel it too.'

'It's like we're being pulled away from our bodies,' said Stephen. 'As if we're on a bit of elastic and it's about to snap.'

'I don't like this at all,' said Kenny.

'Quiet,' said Carol, more abruptly than she intended, if the apology that followed hot on its heels was any indication. 'I'm sorry, Kenny. I didn't mean to be rude, it's just…' she refocused herself, '…there it is.'

'I don't hear anything.' There was strain in John's voice now, as if, back in the Lab, his jaw was clenched.

Carol too spoke with effort.

'It's a sort of pulse. Deep and rhythmic. Like a heartbeat. Try and find it. That's the source.'

There was silence as the other three swept the mental landscape.

'I've got it!' said Stephen triumphantly. Then, less sure: 'I think.'

'No, that's it,' Carol confirmed. 'It's coming in more clearly now, probably because you've tuned into it. Keep focusing. Shut out everything else. Including me.'

Stephen fell silent.

'I've got it too,' said John, a moment later.

'And me,' said Kenny.

'Yes,' said Carol. 'That's it. Now, give it everything you've got. Everything *we've* got.'

In the Lab, their fingers, without breaking contact, spread wide, tendons tightening beneath their skin.

The heartbeat surrounded them now, enveloping them, as though they'd stumbled into an enormous bass drum, just as the band kicked in.

Then, cutting through, the voice. As clear as if it were whispering directly in each of their ears.

'I don't have a choice.'

Carol, true to form, went straight to kindness.

'Can you hear me? We're not here to hurt you. Whatever's happening to you, we can help. You don't have to do anything you don't want to do.'

'Help?' The word was layered with emotions. Fury, terror and self-pity, all at once.

'Go on, Carol,' urged John. 'They're listening, whoever they are.'

'Yes, help,' she said. 'You called us, asked us to stop you. Well, we've come.'

'To help me?'

'Yes, that's right.' She paused before continuing, as if weighing up the ramifications of whatever she said next. 'My name is Carol. And these are my friends – John, Kenny and Stephen. We can be your friends too, if you like.'

The pounding beat seemed to quicken, as if the owner of the voice were excited by the prospect. It did nothing to drown out the reply. This time, however, it came out as an unpleasant hiss.

'This is good.'

'Did that sound good to you, Kenny?' asked Stephen.

'It did not.'

John broke in, a little impatiently.

'We've told you who we are and why we're here. I think it would help us understand what you need if you did the same.'

'What I need?'

'Yes.'

'I need help.'

'So we gathered. What kind of help?'

The heartbeat disappeared abruptly, as though a switch had been thrown or a plug yanked. And for

a second that felt like eternity, the four Tomorrow People experienced silence in its purest form. Neither peace nor quiet, neither stillness nor tranquillity, it was an almost violent soundlessness. Even their own thoughts fled into the dark, leaving their fear without even a means of expression.

Then the voice spoke again, with far more confidence.

'Well, you see,' it said, 'I can't kill them on my own.'

Four heads snapped up simultaneously, the connection severed with brutal swiftness.

Eyes fluttered open and a series of desperate breaths were taken, like swimmers who had lingered underwater too long.

'We're back in the Lab,' said Carol, desperate to hear the sound of any voice other than the one they'd left behind.

'You never left,' TIM reminded her.

'I wouldn't be so sure about that, TIM,' she replied weakly. 'Wherever we were, it certainly wasn't here.'

15

Stephen and Kenny were holding their heads now and groaning softly, but John had leapt straight into action.

'How long, TIM?'

'I'm not sure I understand the question, John.'

'How long were we gone?' He quickly rephrased the question before TIM's pedantry circuits could reactivate. 'How long were we linked?'

'According to my internal chronometer, it has been precisely 1.3 milliseconds since you initiated the psychic link. Was it unsuccessful?'

'You could say that.'

'Who *was* that?' asked Stephen.

'And how can we avoid ever running into them again?' muttered Kenny, rubbing his temples fiercely.

'John...' Carol began,

He held up a hand to stop her.

'I know, Carol.'

'Know what?' demanded Stephen and Kenny in unison. There were very few occasions on which they would tolerate being left out of the loop, and this was none of them.

Not that Carol or John seemed to be paying them much attention.

'But how *can* it be?'

'I don't know.' John paced anxiously. 'I need to think.'

'I really hope you two aren't having the rest of this conversation telepathically,' said Stephen.

'Because that would be rude,' agreed Kenny.

Carol turned to them and the look of utter panic on her face almost made them think twice about wanting an answer.

She gave one anyway.

'I don't know who that was, or what they want. But I'm certain they were human.'

'How do you know?' asked Stephen.

'I could feel it.'

'But you don't know for sure.' Both Kenny and Stephen understood where Carol's line of thinking was leading them, and neither were ready to surrender to it.

'I've learned to trust Carol's feelings when it comes to this sort of thing,' said John. 'To be honest, so have you. If she says that was a human being, then I believe her.'

Stephen threw out one last lifeline.

'And by human being, you mean...'

Carol's expression was sombre.

'No *homo sapiens* I know of have that kind of power.'

The silence that fell over the Lab was less eerie than what they had just experienced, but it was a thin margin.

'If I understand Carol's inference correctly,' said TIM. 'You have just met a new member of *homo superior.*'

'But,' said Stephen, 'they said they were going to kill.'

TIM pondered this briefly.

'That does seem to contradict what we know of the Prime Barrier.'

'And they wanted us to help them,' added Kenny. 'How could we help him, even if we wanted to?' Off a look from Stephen, he held up his hands. 'Which we obviously don't.'

John pursed his lips. He knew it was his job to confront their concerns, come up with a plan and, if at all possible, put things right. That, on this occasion, he hadn't the first idea of how to do any of that was no excuse for not making the attempt.

'Look,' he said, 'it's no good jumping to conclusions. There are still too many missing pieces. The best thing we can do is to track them down in the real world and go from there.'

'But how?' asked Carol.

'That's what I'm trying to work out.'

'Why can't you do the same thing you did with me?' asked Stephen.

'Without knowing their intent, we can't risk anyone reaching out telepathically on their own, which we'd need to do in order to triangulate a position. Isn't that right, TIM?'

'Yes, John, I'm afraid so. But there may be another solution.'

'I'd be happy to hear it.'

'I am not sure that's true.'

TIM's idea was the sort that seemed appallingly simple, provided you didn't think too hard about the specifics. Much of one's life as a Tomorrow Person involved acceptance of what you might once have thought of as outlandish or bizarre. Stephen had come to think of it as 'going with the flow' and this attitude had seen him right so far.

Still, he found himself frowning in concentration as the computer laid out its conclusions.

'As Stephen pointed out, I would ordinarily be able to cross-reference positional data from the field in order to find the location of the original

telepathic signal. As that has been deemed unsafe in this instance, we must rely on the data we do have.'

'What data?' John asked.

'As I stated previously, when Carol first made contact, I was unable to sense a telepathic signal at work. When you made your joint attempt, this continued to be true. I have only your own accounts of the experience to work from.'

Stephen sighed. 'Then we don't have anything to go on!'

'Untrue, Stephen. I theorise that something or someone was blocking my own telepathic abilities, either with deliberate intent or as a side effect of the development of their powers.'

John drummed his fingers against the tabletop thoughtfully.

'That makes sense, TIM, but how does it help us?'

'Each of you described a pulse, a heartbeat that led you to the psychic connection. The more attuned you became to your... correspondent... the more intense that sound became.'

'It's true,' said Carol. 'It was there from the first time I became aware that something was out there. A thump, then a pulse; then, like you say, a sort of heartbeat.'

'I suggest, Carol, that the truth is more prosaic than we have assumed.'

'What do you mean?'

'Have you heard the Earth expression, *wearing one's heart on one's sleeve*?'

Kenny demurred. 'You think we were hearing their actual heartbeat?'

Whatever John had been expecting TIM to come up with, it wasn't this.

'That's never happened before, TIM.'

'As Carol pointed out, we are working from a limited dataset when it comes to the first flowering of telepathic ability. And there is some evidence in my databanks, concerning other telepathic races, that lends credence to my hypothesis. On one planet, for instance, telepaths are available to transmit odours alongside their thoughts.'

Kenny surreptitiously sniffed at his jacket and wrinkled his nose.

'All right,' said John, 'let's assume you're correct.'

'A sensible assumption,' offered TIM.

He ignored that and continued:

'We all heard the heartbeat. How does that enable us to track them?'

'I will need access to your memories of that heartbeat.'

21

'All right.'

'And then we will need the assistance of Mister Harding and Mister Leftridge.'

An hour later, the Lab had taken on even more of a 'mad scientist's lair' atmosphere than usual.

Ginge, in particular, was less than taken with the new arrangements.

'Here,' he said miserably, 'if this is your way of getting back at us for the way we met, then I'd like to offer evidence of how much we've helped you since.'

'It was all Ginge's idea,' said Lefty. 'I knew that Jedikiah bloke was trouble from the off.'

'Stop moaning,' said Kenny. 'We're all in the same boat.'

It was true. None of them looked particularly comfortable. They stood in a rough semi-circle around the Lab table, the four Tomorrow People and their human friends, each with a series of sensors attached to their clothing, long translucent wires leading into one of TIM's many control surfaces.

Ginge and Lefty, in their biker gear, always seemed somewhat out of place in the high-tech Lab,

but, to their credit, they had been incredibly loyal friends to the Tomorrow People once they'd given up kidnapping them. And, for all they were complaining now, they'd still agreed to help, despite not entirely understanding what was being asked of them.

'There's nothing to worry about,' said John, hoping that was true. 'TIM simply needs to create a small sample of *homo sapiens* and *homo superior* heartbeats.'

'Oh, is that all?' Ginge was unplacated. 'And what if the power goes out while we're connected up to all this?'

'I am not connected to the national grid, Mister Harding. My power will not go out.'

'But you admit that would be a bad thing.'

'The process will be painless.'

'My dentist always say that,' chipped in Lefty. 'And he's always wrong.'

'TIM, perhaps we had best just get on with it.'

'Of course, Carol. Commencing recording.'

The wires leading to Lefty's chest lit up, drawing a yelp from the smaller of the two humans. Soon, the room was filled with the sound of his heartbeat, quickened by anxiety but steady and strong. The sound and light disappeared swiftly, and the process was repeated with Ginge.

23

'It would be preferable to have a greater number of *homo sapiens* heartbeats as a control group,' said TIM, 'but I should be able to extrapolate potential variables.'

'Great,' said Ginge, plucking sensors from his vest and T-shirt, 'I'd hate for you not to be able to elaborate your vegetables.'

'Now us,' instructed John.

'Are our heartbeats so different?' asked Stephen.

'We're a new species, remember,' answered Carol. 'There are bound to be differences we're not even aware of. Isn't that right, TIM?'

'That's right. Your powers are not the only thing about you that has evolved. The hope is that we should be able to isolate those differences by cross-referencing them with those of Mister Harding and Mister Leftridge.'

One by one, the Tomorrow People's heartbeats were summoned into the room. On first listen, they all sounded very much the same, if immediately a little more robust than their sap friends.

'Not bad,' judged Kenny, on hearing his own. 'Couldn't dance to it though.'

'Yeah.' Stephen grinned. 'Bit young for the slow ones, aren't you?'

'And you're not?' Carol said, with a twinkle.

'Laugh it up,' countered Ginge. 'I'm still not sure we haven't just been taken for mugs.'

The bio-fluid in TIM's tubes flowed as lights of various hues flickered across the Lab. It felt as though the entire room were thinking and, in many ways, it was.

'I think we have all that we need.'

Everyone, now free of wiring, stepped forward to the table, not entirely sure what to expect.

A hologrammatic map of London appeared, overlaid with a sea with blinking red dots. There were so many that, at first, it appeared to be a single, pulsing sea.

'We're sure they're here?' Stephen passed a hand through the map, the light breaking and shimmering over his fingers. 'In London, I mean.'

'They felt close,' said Carol. And they had. Painfully so. That being said, she also didn't want to imagine the consequences of the voice's owner being powerful enough to reach out over larger distances, especially if they were only just breaking out. What would that mean for them in full possession of their powers?

'First,' purred TIM, 'we shall attempt to remove *homo sapiens* heartbeats from the map. I have amplified my own telepathic transmitters to pinpoint

the location of each member of the populace. Then, using the data from our *homo sapiens* friends, I have translated those neural feeds into biological output.'

'What they're thinking can tell you how their hearts are beating?' Stephen gave a whistle. He didn't understand a word of it, but it was undeniably impressive.

'Within an acceptable margin of error. For instance, I was able to deduce a range of changes in Mister Harding's and Mister Leftridge's heartbeats occasioned by their trepidation and, in Mister Harding's case, extreme annoyance.'

'Let's see how you'd feel if I attached wires to you!'

'There are several thousand wires attached to me,' TIM pointed out. 'A fact that has not, as yet, occasioned any discomfort.'

'TIM,' said John. 'I think we get the gist. What happens when you remove the *homo sapiens* from the map?'

The map flickered briefly and much of the red vanished, leaving behind one small cluster, in what everyone immediately assumed to be a certain Lab in a certain disused London Underground tunnel.

'That's us!'

'That's right, Kenny.'

And, worryingly nearby, a solitary red dot, pulsing slowly. Almost ominously.

No one spoke for a long moment. It was difficult to decide whether TIM's plan having worked was better or worse than the alternative.

'Can you show us exactly where they are?' asked John.

'Yes, John.'

The map expanded and unfolded, moving from the computerised display to an astonishingly detailed colour photograph of a large, six storey building. Stone-fronted and lined with small windows.

'Where on Earth's that?' asked Kenny.

Carol gave a gasp of recognition. John instinctively moved to her side.

'What is it, Carol?'

'It's a police station. In Leman Street. The new building only opened a few years ago. I read about it in the newspaper.'

'I think I'll pass on getting involved with the Old Bill,' said Ginge, 'if it's all the same to you.'

'The new building?' John pressed on.

'Yes, there's been a police station there for almost a hundred years. Since the time of…'

Carol brushed the thought off. It was a coincidence, nothing more.

'Since the time of what?'

She couldn't quite bring herself to say it; TIM had no such compunctions.

'Since the time, John, of Jack the Ripper.'

Episode Two

Just over an hour later, John and Carol stepped onto the jaunting pad. It hadn't taken long to come up with a workable plan, although there had been considerable discussion as to the wisdom of it.

'Is everyone clear on what they need to do?'

Stephen shrugged.

'You're going to jaunt into Jack the Ripper's place and we're going to wait and see if you live long enough to send further instructions.'

'And if you don't,' quipped Kenny, 'we pack a bag and go on a long holiday. In hyperspace.'

'It's not Jack the Ripper's *place*, Stephen.' Carol's tone was intended to calm, but she wasn't entirely certain it was directed outwards. 'There's simply a historical connection.'

'And a creepy voice talking about killing people.'

'Hopefully that's simply a... misunderstanding.'

'Yeah,' said Kenny, dryly, 'I'm sure they didn't mean *kill* in a *bad* way.'

'The sooner we get in there,' interjected John, a little impatiently, 'the sooner we'll know exactly what we're dealing with.'

Stephen held back a mutter of *that's what I'm afraid of* and, instead, went with: 'Good luck.'

'To all of us,' replied John. Then, to TIM: 'We're ready.'

'Of course, John.'

As they vanished, Kenny turned to Stephen.

'I hope they know what they're doing.'

Trying desperately to lighten the mood, his friend gave him a playful punch on the arm.

'Why should any of us start now?'

Ginge and Lefty were already on their way to the police station, by more conventional means.

After their ordeal in the Lab, it felt comfortingly normal to be on their bikes on the open road, the wind in their hair and the sun high over their heads. Ginge knew the feeling wouldn't last long; it wouldn't take them more than another half an hour

to reach their destination and whatever awaited them there. So he decided he was going to enjoy it.

Just in case he didn't get the chance again.

On the whole, since joining forces with the Tomorrow People, Ginge had felt much better about himself and about life in general. He'd always seen himself as someone with a part to play, someone destined for great things. For a very long time, no one – at home or at the school he'd sporadically attended – had seemed to share his conviction, which is probably why he had proved such an easy mark for Jedikiah. But now he knew that, while he might not be part of the great evolutionary leap forward that his friends represented, he was no longer just a face in the crowd. He was a part of making things better.

That couldn't be bad. Even if it occasionally meant riding into the sort of trouble he was headed for now.

He glanced over at Lefty, riding alongside him. Best mate he could ever have, but not exactly the sharpest tool in the shed. Still, sometimes he envied his… simplicity. Lefty was always happy to help and someone you definitely wanted on your side when the chips were down, but Ginge doubted that his friend had given much thought to the change in

their circumstances other than that John and the rest of the team shouted at him significantly less often than Jedikiah had. And the grub was better.

Must be nice, thought Ginge, to have such easily fulfilled aspirations.

Thirty minutes later, they pulled up outside Leman Street Police Station and parked up their bikes.

It had been a good long while since Ginge had been in a police station and entering one voluntarily would be an entirely new experience. The task they had been set, however, was entirely in his wheelhouse.

Lefty's hand went to the strap of his helmet, but Ginge stopped him before he could unfasten it.

'Leave it on,' he said. 'This is war. Let's stay in uniform.'

The desk sergeant's name was McCourt, and he had been on duty for two hours longer than his patience had held out (and three more than any sane man could have maintained benevolence for the human race).

It was only the middle of the afternoon and he'd already been complained at by half a dozen locals about an admittedly overzealous traffic warden working the area, had been forced to explain to one woman that the current whereabouts of her Yorkshire Terrier did not, precisely, fall under the jurisdiction of the Metropolitan Police and, in the interim, fielded several crank calls claiming to know the identity of the true culprits behind the Baker Street robbery, despite or, more likely because of, the trial having ended several months previously.

Had he been English, he might, perhaps, simply have imposed upon a passing constable for another cup of builder's tea and suffered in silence. Being a son of Caledonia, however, he had, beneath his breath, grown downright poetic in his invective towards the public in general and, more specifically, the current occupants of East London and their mothers.

He was therefore, in no mood for the appearance of the two young men, in motorcycling attire, who burst through the door of the station, shouted something about a revolution and started flinging chairs about.

Sergeant McCourt walked out from behind his desk and made his way, calmly, towards the larger of the two. Years of experience had taught

him to recognise the brains of any given operation, although, on this occasion, he was fairly certain he'd have made the same choice with his head in a bag.

'Can I help you?'

He was a big lad, without a doubt, but McCourt was bigger. Not that this fact seemed to put a dent in the biker's confidence.

'I want to see the Chief Constable!' he bellowed.

'Yeah!' offered his sidekick, by way of support.

Down the adjacent corridor, doors were already beginning to open, the promise of impending drama attracting weary officers like moths to a flame. Some of them were simply happy enough for a brief respite from stacks of overdue paperwork, others had earlier witnessed the desk sergeant spend half an hour taking down the details of a stolen watch that was visibly present on the wrist of the man making the complaint and had a book running on when he would finally reach the end of his tether.

'Chief Constable's at New Scotland Yard. He tends to be. What with him being Chief Constable. Now why don't you step away from the chairs? They've done nothing to you.'

'But I have information.'

'I'm sure you do.'

'It's important.'

McCourt removed his glasses and rubbed wearily at the bridge of his nose.

'Let me guess. The Baker Street robbery?'

Caught off-guard, the young man's face clouded briefly, but his partner's head quickly appeared over his shoulder, apparently eager to contribute something to the conversation. 'Yeah, that's right! It's a stitch-up!'

The first biker smiled ingratiatingly at the Sergeant.

'You heard him. We've got the real story for you.'

'Right then,' said the Sergeant, throwing a warning glance towards the officers gathered, delightedly, in the corridor. 'I'll get a pencil, shall I?'

John and Carol had jaunted into the close confines of a broom closet, causing an unexpected clatter of brooms and mops that made them both wince. Through the closed door, they could hear the commotion of Ginge and Lefty's arrival.

Telepathically, John reached out to the Lab.

'TIM, can you hear me? I don't think we've much time.'

'I can hear you, John.'

'Are we close?'

'Yes, according to my readings, the subject is being held in an interview room, one room to your left.'

Carol, listening in, opened the door a crack and peered out. As they'd hoped, the brief distraction had cleared them a path to their quarry.

'Thank you, TIM. We'll report in as soon as we can.'

Together, they crept silently into the corridor, away from the mass of rubbernecking police, and moved swiftly towards the next door along.

It was unlocked, which should have been a moment of celebration, but they still had no idea what they would find on the other side of it.

'Come on, John,' Carol's voice floated into his mind. 'Before we think better of it.'

John grasped the handle and pushed.

Whatever or whoever they had been expecting, it wasn't Abel Brown.

The boy slumped in the wooden chair, on one side of a long, slightly wobbly table, looked impossibly young, no more than 13. Thin to the point of malnourishment, he was clad only in a grubby white T-shirt and jeans and looked utterly

terrified. No one's idea, then, of a malevolent force of nature.

His eyes widened as John and Carol entered, shoving the door closed behind them.

'Who are you?' he sputtered.

Abel had spent the best part of the day fielding increasingly aggressive questions from one set of police officers, and overly accommodating enquiries from another. Did he realise how much trouble he was in? Couldn't he spare a thought for the parents? Was he warm enough? Did he want tea? A biscuit?

If they'd hoped either approach would get him to open up, they were mistaken. He was tired, scared and, what's more, failed to see what any of this had to do with him. As far as Abel was concerned, he was suffering the after-effects of someone's appalling mistake.

The rather trendy-looking young people before him did nothing to relieve those feelings. He wondered if this was a new trick, sending in someone his own age to have another run at him.

He tried to remember the breathing exercises Mr Richardson had taught him, for when his stage fright was at its worst, or his headaches got too bad.

He'd only just managed to inhale, when Carol rushed over.

'Do you recognise my voice?' she asked.

Abel shook his head.

'Should I?'

'Possibly,' she said. 'But let's not worry about that now. We're here to help.'

John watched the boy carefully for any reaction that might suggest they were speaking to the same person they'd encountered earlier.

'I just want to go home.' Abel looked as if he might burst into tears at any moment.

There was a faint sound of movement from beyond the door. Officers reluctantly returning to their work.

'Carol,' said John, 'we're running out of time.'

'What's your name?' the young woman asked the boy, making her voice as soft as she could, under the circumstances.

'Abel. Abel Brown.'

'Good, that's good. Hello Abel. I'm Carol. Are you *sure* you don't remember me at all?'

Abel's lip began to tremble. Carol laid a gentle hand on his shoulder.

'How about now?'

The boy stared back at her, his distress turning to utter amazement. Her lips hadn't moved, but he had heard her all the same.

'How are you doing that?' he blurted. It took a moment for him to realise that he hadn't spoken aloud either.

'Did you hear that, John?'

'I did.'

Abel felt a prickle of fresh horror run up his spine. What has happening? They were having a whole conversation, but no one had said a word.

'TIM?'

'Yes, John?'

Abel glanced around wildly. Who was Tim? *Where* was Tim?

'We're ready to jaunt back. And we'll be bringing a guest.' John joined Carol at Abel's side, and without further ado, lifted the boy from the chair and hoisted him over his shoulder. He was even lighter than John had expected and it nearly unbalanced him.

As did the shocked Abel's wriggling.

'What are you doing? Put me down!' he shouted,

failing to make use of the privacy that telepathy allowed them.

As if in response, there was a knock on the door.

'Quiet, Abel, please,' urged Carol, in the boy's mind.

The intensity of her plea, in concert with Abel's exhaustion, seemed to achieve what strategy alone could not. Abruptly, he fell still and silent.

Carol felt a pang of concern.

'I think he's passed out.'

'All the more reason to get him back to the Lab as soon as possible.'

'Who's in there?' a voice demanded gruffly. 'Connolly, if you think you can toady up to the Superintendent by breaking the kid first…'

The aggrieved officer seemed willing to wait for an answer, turning the door handle even as he made his accusation.

John's eyes flicked to the door, shoving it back into the frame with his mind and, for good measure, locking it tight.

The knocking became a banging.

'Open this door, or I swear…'

'Now would be a good time, TIM.'

John, Carol and the limp body of Abel Brown shimmered onto the Lab's jaunting pad.

Stephen and Kenny, who had been hovering anxiously at its edge both took an immediate step backwards. John pushed past them and, as gently as he could, laid Abel out on the table.

'Is he conscious?' asked Carol, stepping from the pad. It was unclear to whom she'd directed the question, John or Tim, but the computer answered first.

'All life signs appear normal.'

'And is he....'

The London map shimmered back to life. A single cluster of red dots – five heartbeats – in a single location.

'It would certainly appear so, Carol.'

Stephen and Kenny, having decided that there was no imminent threat of carnage, moved in for a closer look. They weren't overly impressed.

'That's who we've been so worried about? He looks like a stiff breeze would do him in!'

'Or Kenny,' Stephen chimed in.

'Shut up, you.'

John and Carol exchanged a glance. At that precise moment, they'd happily take whatever reassuring shards of normality were on offer.

'So,' asked Stephen, returning to the matter at hand, 'is he a Tomorrow Person or not?'

'We still don't know,' admitted John.

'He's telepathic,' said Carol, 'but he didn't seem to recognise us at all. Or understand what was going on.'

Kenny had another question, one none of them had thought to ask thus far.

'Why was he in the police station in the first place?'

John was just about to acknowledge the point when the words 'police station' tugged his thoughts in another direction entirely.

With a groan, he leapt back onto the jaunting pad.

'Stephen,' he ordered. 'Come with me.'

'What? Why?'

'We've forgotten something rather important.'

42

Sergeant McCourt pulled the heavy steel door closed behind him, glanced at his watch, then marched down the corridor towards the officers' locker room, feeling much cheerier than he had earlier.

He did not believe for a moment that the cell's new occupants were actually called Ted Heath and Harold Wilson, as they claimed, but they'd have time to think about it overnight and, best of all, be someone else's problem come the morning.

As for McCourt, there was a warm bottle and a warmer bed waiting for him at home. And, if he was lucky, a dream of a simpler life, perhaps at sea, without miscreants to manage or reports to file.

By the time he'd changed into his civvies, he was whistling.

There was less cause for celebration inside the cell.

'Was this part of the plan, Ginge?'

Lefty laid back on the narrow bench that ran along the back wall, examining his fingernails. He didn't seem overly concerned that they'd just been locked up, a feeling that Ginge couldn't bring himself to share.

He tried to pace, if only to use up nervous energy, but it was too confined a space. In the end, he made do with shifting his weight from leg to leg and gritting his teeth.

'I'll be honest, Lefty,' he admitted reluctantly, 'I never thought to ask. I assumed that lot would have something clever up their sleeves.'

This answer suited Lefty as much as any other and he folded his hands behind his head and shut his eyes. If there was a better excuse for a quick kip, he'd not encountered it yet.

'That's what I thought,' he murmured sleepily. 'Let me know when they turn up.'

If they turn up, thought Ginge. The trouble with clever people, in his experience, was that simple things often flew clean out of their heads.

He looked at the now slumbering Lefty.

Simple things and their mates.

He'd built up quite a good head of steam on the subject of the supposedly more evolved and their lack of manner, where the cell door flew open and he was greeted by a grinning Stephen.

'Didn't think we'd forgotten you, did you?'

Behind him, a gratifyingly sheepish John avoided the biker's gaze.

'Of course not,' said Ginge, with all the dignity

at his disposal. 'I mean, what would you do without me?'

He turned and nudged Lefty awake.

'Come on, you lump. Cavalry's here.'

A quick jaunt landed the four of them next to the parked bikes. Ginge released himself from John's grasp and straightened his vest. It wasn't what you would call a dignified way to travel, he thought, not for the first time, but it did the job.

'Thanks for putting together the rescue party,' he said, with genuine gratitude. Although he quickly threw in an 'eventually' for the sake of his pride.

'Hey,' said Stephen brightly, as Lefty slouched away from him to check the bikes for interference. 'we have to look after our pet Saps, don't we?'

Ginge glowered good-naturedly.

'Funny thing about pets,' he threw back. 'Sometimes, they bite.'

'We appreciate the help, as always,' said John. 'So, what next?'

'We need to get back to the Lab. We may have a new Tomorrow Person on our hands.'

'What was he doing in the nick, anyway? I thought your lot were all do-gooder types.'

'Kenny had the same question. And it's a good one.'

'Maybe he's just more fun that the rest of you.'

Before John could respond, he heard TIM's voice in his mind.

'Have you retrieved Mister Harding and Mister Leftridge?'

'Yes, TIM. All safe and sound. We're about to head back.'

'You might consider delaying your return. I have been looking into the reasons for our new friend's incarceration and the results are, to say the least, disturbing. I think you may need to investigate further.'

'All right. What have you got so far?'

John's face grew ashen as TIM shared his discoveries. Even Stephen, who had, up to this point, only been half-heartedly paying attention, seemed shaken.

'Not a scratch,' said Lefty happily, strolling back to the group. He cast his eyes over John and Stephen, who both stood frighteningly still as they took in whatever they were hearing.

'Now, I can't read minds, Lefty,' said Ginge,

'but does it look like they're getting good news to you?'

Back at the Lab, Abel had regained consciousness and was sitting across the table from Carol. TIM had produced a warm cup of cocoa, the only refreshment that had seemed to interest the boy, seemingly from thin air and Kenny, although not without complaint, had fetched him a blanket, before settling himself into the corner with a comic book.

'Just so you know,' he said, as he flipped through the pages, 'I think you're mad. He's never one of us.'

'You're welcome to jaunt to the others,' she'd told him, but he'd said he was perfectly happy where he was. He wanted to be there, he insisted, when he was proved right. By which, Carol knew, he really meant he was going to stay and look out for her, for which she was grateful.

Abel seemed calmer than he had at the police station. In some ways, this worried Carol more. It was a perilously thin line between calm and catatonic, especially on the cusp of breaking out.

She had been there when Stephen had gone through the process and it had taken a concerted effort to keep him from slipping away. The dangers of an unguided transition were very real: a person could jaunt themselves into the sea, or inside a brick wall, before they realised what they were doing. Or, worse still, they could disappear into their own minds, with no way back to the conscious world. Forever floating. Alive but not alive.

John, the only one of them who had made the transition without help, had been very lucky and it had been a close call even then. And he, especially, had sworn that no one else would have to do it alone.

Yet now, finally faced with the opportunity to help another Tomorrow Person achieve their destiny, she hesitated. The echo of that dark voice, though she struggled to believe it belonged to Abel, still lingered. And the fragmented information TIM had gleaned by hacking into the station's telephone systems hadn't done much to reassure her. It might have helped if they'd had more than rudimentary computer systems, but while there was talk of a Police National Computer, it had not yet gone live, and, for TIM, would undoubtedly have been like interrogating an abacus.

What they had managed to piece together from various conversations and a handful of uncharacteristically circumspect newspaper articles was this:

Five people had been reported missing over the course of the previous two months. All young people, between the ages of 12 and 16. The police had kept, and continued to keep, the connection between these disappearances quiet, in order to prevent a public panic.

Or, more likely, a public outcry. The involvement of a previous incarnation of Leman Street Station with some of the most famous unsolved crimes of the previous century would not go unnoticed if the press ever got hold of the entire jigsaw. Whitechapel was still a word with the power to chill.

Every effort to locate any of the missing children had proved fruitless so far and there was a growing sense of foreboding, a creeping suspicion that they might never be found alive. The overwhelming mood amongst the police was frustration, even desperation.

Until, that is, some piece of evidence, though TIM had not yet managed to identify what, had led them to Abel Brown.

The unlikely prime suspect. Who, if he was a Tomorrow Person, thought Carol, ought to have

possessed another 'prime' that would rule him out. Of taking lives, at any rate.

John and Stephen had stayed in the field, with Ginge and Lefty, trying to see what else – if anything – they could learn about the case. While she sought answers directly from Abel Brown.

She looked into the young boy's eyes, searching for anything, anything at all, that would convince her that she was looking at a kidnapper or, worse, a killer.

All she saw was a scared young man.

Who needed her.

'Abel,' she whispered, her eyes locked on his. When he tried to look away, she reached out and took hold of both of his hands. 'I need you to listen to me. I know you're confused and scared but I promise, you're quite safe.'

'Where are we?'

'It's called the Lab, but we'll talk about that later. For the moment, I want you to concentrate on what I'm telling you. And look carefully into my eyes.'

Abel blinked away fresh tears but did as she asked.

'Now, do you trust me?'

'Yes,' Abel replied. And he did, completely, though he couldn't have said why.

'Good. Now, I want you to do something. I want you to try to relax and imagine that your mind… is a fist. A great, big fist, clenched tight.'

Images were beginning to flood into the boy's mind. He could see it. His own hand, bathed in fluorescent light, disconnected from the rest of his body. And other scenes too, skipping across his vision like the stereoscopic pictures in the View-Master he'd once been given for Christmas. An infant, curled into a ball. Flowers, planets, stars. Infinite galaxies. Infinite possibilities.

'Now,' Carol urged, 'let it open, slowly. Don't let any other thoughts come into your head. Just think of the fist, opening very slowly. Like a flower.'

'I can feel you,' whispered Abel. 'Inside my head. Like before, at the station, but… stronger somehow.'

'That's good. Hold onto that feeling. And try to talk to me in your mind, like you did then.'

He focused again on the fist, unclenching, relaxing, then cast his next thought towards Carol.

'What's happening to me?'

Carol smiled. No matter what else happened, this was a beautiful moment, one that some part of her had feared she'd never experience again.

'You're becoming one of us.'

Abel saw his own face in his mind. At peace, eyes closed against all the terrible things in the world, looking inward towards everything good and pure.

'Who's us?'

'The Tomorrow People,' said Carol. 'You're becoming one of the Tomorrow People.'

'Yes,' Abel said telepathically, a wave of serenity washing over him. 'I understand.' His mind was opening, reaching out in all directions. He felt a surge of power travel the lengths of his limbs, felt himself become both weightless and grounded in a way he had never experienced before. He was connected. All around him, inside him, unfamiliar sensations calling out for him, beckoning to him to come and experience them.

Overwhelming them all, was a slow, steady pulse, like a heartbeat. Its voice was the loudest. It needed him to follow it, to fold himself into its embrace. All he needed to do was let go.

Carol heard it too, a fraction too late. Felt the boy jerk away from her, as his mind surrendered itself to the pulse.

'No, Abel,' she said aloud, tightening her grip on his hands. 'You mustn't. It's not safe.'

Kenny threw down his comic and leapt forward.

'Carol, what is it?' He tried to reach into her mind, to hear for himself what was happening, but something slapped him away.

'TIM! Can you hear them?'

'No, Kenny. I cannot.'

'What do I do?'

'I am trying to contact John and Stephen, but it seems I am currently unable to make any connections.'

'Abel,' the dark voice repeated slowly, as if it were trying the name on for size. 'Yes. I am Abel.'

'No, you are *not*.' She reached out desperately for the boy's actual mind, but something powerful slammed against her own, like a wave, and sent her consciousness spinning.

A scream forced its way from her throat. Kenny tried to run to her, but an energy field of some kind had been thrown up, surrounding Carol and the

boy. He was thrown backwards, landing heavily against the far wall. Groaning, he stumbled back to his feet.

'We have to do something, TIM!'

The computer's voice was as placid as ever, even as its systems ran thousands of scenarios a second, searching for a solution.

To no avail.

'I fear we must let Carol do what she can. She is not incapable.'

Not incapable but certainly struggling.

'Who else would I be?' the voice insisted. 'Who else *could* I be? I am Abel and Abel is me.' A sinister chuckle followed, as though it were amused by its own inadvertent rhyme scheme.

Using all of her willpower, Carol grasped control, grounding herself to her body, to Abel's body, to her task.

'Let him go!'

'Imagine your mind is a fist, Carol.'

'Stop it.'

Abel's hands began to grow hot beneath hers,

yet still she held on. Her head felt like it were in a vice.

'No, I have a better idea. Imagine *my* mind is a fist.'

'I don't know who you are or what you want…' she shouted.

The voice interrupted her.

'I am Abel,' it growled. 'And I want… everything.'

Episode Three

A blanket of silence lay over the Lab.

Silence and darkness.

If anyone had been conscious to see it, it would have felt uncomfortably like a tomb; the two figures that could be made out, just, were sprawled awkwardly on the ground, their bodies contorted into unnatural positions.

A small miracle then, when one of them stirred.

'Kenny,' Carol murmured, as she returned gingerly to the world. 'Kenny, are you all right?' There was no answer. She tried again, this time telepathically. There was an encouraging glimmer of activity, even if he was not yet conscious enough to answer; she pulled herself to her feet and groped her way towards his crumpled form.

Instinctively, she also tried to reach out to TIM, albeit without much hope. The computer's systems

appeared to have been completely deactivated and she wasn't sure she'd know where to start in addressing that. She needed to find John. He'd built TIM, after all.

Not that she could contact him at present. Whatever Abel – or Abel's... the word *passenger* kept insinuating itself into her mind – had done, her powers seemed, at present, to be contained to the Lab itself. Which meant no jaunting to safety, either. She and Kenny would have to find their way to the surface the old-fashioned way.

Hopefully a solution would occur to her on the way.

She kneeled at Kenny's side and placed two fingers firmly on the side of his neck, breathing a sigh of relief at the robust pulse.

Multiple questions wrestled for pole position in her thoughts, if precious few answers. That heartbeat, the one they'd all heard now, was the key to the mystery, she was sure of it. What it meant, or to whom it actually belonged, remained unclear.

It wasn't Abel Brown, that much she knew. Not in the way they'd first imagined, anyway. It was tied to the boy, it was inside him, but it was so diametrically opposed to the personality she'd

sensed during their link that she couldn't see it as the same person, whatever claims it had made.

And there was more. As Abel had lost control of his thoughts, his memories had spilled out, giving Carol much more access to his inner life than she'd have taken without permission.

Much of it was terribly sad. Abel had been orphaned when he was eight years old – courtesy of a rain-soaked night, a hairpin turn and a careless driver – and had spent the last five years of his life in a series of foster homes. Never quite fitting in, though he was seldom in one place long enough to make the attempt.

There were a few happy memories though, which had felt quite recent, though they had been harder to get a handle on. The darkness kept rising to the surface.

His health had been a constant issue, especially the splitting headaches that seemed to have beleaguered him over the last few years. Those could, Carol thought, be attributed to beginning to break out – all four of them had experienced similar symptoms – but the longstanding nature of the condition lent her doubts.

The essential problem remained how little they knew about the variables. Their own journeys on the

way to becoming Tomorrow People had been deeply personal, but with sufficient common factors to feel like a shared experience.

They'd certainly not faced anything like this. Any strange voices they'd heard had belonged to each other and had been there to ease their passage.

Was Abel's dark alter ego an internal or external force? If external, where had it come from and why had it attached itself to the boy? Because of his burgeoning abilities?

If internal, if somehow a part of Abel himself, why were its murderous intentions unaffected by the Prime Barrier?

Neither scenario contained much comfort, so Carol was doubly appreciative that Kenny chose that moment to open his eyes and push himself up onto his elbows.

He took in the darkened Lab and grunted.

'I hate to say *I told you so,* but…'

Carol couldn't help but smile. She helped him to his feet.

'You love to say *I told you so.*'

'True.'

'But you'll have to gloat later. We need to get out of here and find the others.'

'What about TIM?'

Carol pushed the worst case scenario away.

'We'll sort TIM out, don't worry.'

'And the kid?'

The *kid* in question was at least a year older than Kenny, but Carol let that pass.

'I honestly don't know. He could be anywhere. And without TIM, I'm not sure how we're going to find him again. Unless he wants us to.'

'Oh, he wants us to.'

'What do you mean?'

'He, or it, or whatever, came looking for us, remember. Whatever he's up to, he wants us to be a part of it.'

A thought struck Carol. 'But that's not the first message I received, was it? The first message was *Stop me, before I do it again.* The voice I heard in Abel's mind before,' she gestured at the lifeless Lab, 'all this... did not want to be stopped.'

'So, how many people have we been talking to?'

Carol shrugged.

'I'm more concerned right now about what happens now they're talking to each other.'

An hour or so earlier, John and Stephen had sent Ginge and Lefty on their way. 'Early release for good behaviour,' Ginge had called it, though he extracted a promise from John to get in touch if they needed further help.

Then they'd set to attempting to find a connection, any connection, between the missing children, in the hopes that it might give them a clue as to what had actually happened to them.

'I wonder how Carol's getting on,' Stephen mused.

'I'm sure she'll let us know soon enough,' replied John. 'I don't want to disturb her if we can help it. Helping someone to break out can be a delicate procedure under the best of circumstances, as I'm sure you remember.' He stopped outside the door of an ordinary-looking terraced house. 'And these are far from the best of circumstances.'

'Are we going to knock?'

'And say what? I don't think we're likely to get the parents to tell us much. We hardly look like police officers.'

'Junior detectives?' He looked down at his jumper and jeans. 'Plain clothes? Undercover?'

'We'd have to be very junior indeed. No, I think the best thing to do is to get into the missing child's bedroom and take a look around.'

John considered the upper floor windows, focusing on the one to the right. Its curtains were conveniently open and he could make out posters for two or three well-known bands on the walls.

'That looks a likely suspect. And a short jaunt.'

'What if someone's in there?'

'You're right. One of us had best cause a distraction.'

'Ah, so we are going undercover, after all.'

'I am. I need you to nip up there and gather what evidence you can. Photographs. Journals. That sort of thing. Anything can give us some insight into their life before this happened.'

'I'll see what I can find.'

John marched up to the front door and knocked. Hearing approaching footsteps, he reached out to his friend.

'Now!'

Stephen gave a little salute and disappeared in a flicker of light.

After a moment, a woman appeared. It was clear she hadn't slept much and appeared to have been crying.

'Mrs Haynes?'

The woman pulled a handkerchief from her sleeve and dabbed at her grief-reddened nose.

'Yes?'

'My name is John Dixon. I'm a friend of Mary's.'

'Oh. From the theatre?'

John hedged his bets, 'Yes, that's right. I don't mean to disturb you, but the whole... troupe have been so terribly upset by what's happened, and, well, I just wondered if there was anything I could do. To help out.'

'I'm just glad to hear she's made friends there,' Mrs Haynes looked as if she might cry again. 'She wasn't at all sure about going at first. But we've moved around so often and it's so been difficult for her to get her bearings. Forever changing schools and so on. We thought if she got involved in an activity...' Now the tears did start to fall.

John felt a twinge of discomfort. He'd have been much happier upstairs hunting for evidence and there was no doubt Stephen was better at this sort of thing.

But it was his responsibility and that was something he took very seriously.

He reached out and took her hand.

'I assure you. We all liked her very much.' He regretted the last sentence even as it came out of his mouth. 'I should say, we all *like* her very much, and we're very much hoping for her safe return.'

63

'You're a very kind, young man. I don't think there's anything you can do, but please don't think I don't appreciate the offer.'

'I'm ready when you are.' Stephen's voice in John's mind was a welcome relief from the volume of the woman's pain. He tried not to let it show.

'That's quite all right, Mrs Haynes. We just wanted you to know that you're not alone.'

And, John thought, if it was within his power, her daughter would be returned to her.

'Thank you. And please thank Mary's other... friends for me. And that nice Mr Richardson.'

'I will.'

With a small, sad smile, Mrs Haynes closed the door.

John waited for the footsteps to recede, then quickly signalled his friend.

'All clear.'

A moment later Stephen reappeared beside him and handed over a pile of papers and photos.

'Excellent work, Constable Jameson.'

'Thank you, Inspector Dixon. Did you learn anything from the mother?'

'I'm not sure yet. Perhaps.'

'Four more kids to scout out,' Stephen reminded him. 'I hope you can stay in character that long.'

'Funny you should say that.'

Carol and Kenny reached the surface, aching and out of breath, after about fifteen minutes. Every step had felt like walking through molasses, as though the Lab, or whatever had been in the Lab, hadn't wanted them to leave.

Now, it felt like they'd run a marathon. A little less jaunting in future, Carol promised herself, a little more walking. Even *homo superior* needed to get their exercise, though she had a feeling they'd get their fair share of activity in before this was finished.

First, it was time to test the full extent of the damage to her powers.

'John?'

The answer came almost immediately, brightening her mood considerably.

'Carol. Thank goodness. We've been trying to reach you. Has something happened?'

'You could say that.'

'Is Kenny with you?'

'Yeah, I'm here.'

'Good. Can you get to us? We've managed to make some progress, although we could certainly use your help.'

'Tell us where you are and we'll find you. Though I'm a little anxious about jaunting long distances. TIM is currently… offline.'

Carol heard the concern in John's voice, though he quickly covered it.

'Well, the belts have been working for us, so far. But, just to be safe, let's meet somewhere familiar. Somewhere you can picture.'

'All right, but where?'

'Stephen's house. We've all been there. Is that all right with you, Stephen?'

'Sure,' he chimed in. 'Mum's probably out, anyway. Not that she'd mind.'

Stephen's mother had never been entirely comfortable with her son's new life with the Tomorrow People but, for the most part, neither she nor her husband had made much fuss about it, provided Stephen's school reports remained good, which they did.

Despite having seen something of the powers that their son now possessed and every attempt he'd made to be transparent about his adventures, Stephen had long ago realised that his parents treated the whole thing as just another extracurricular activity, like fencing, and was sure they secretly hoped it would somehow stand him in good stead when it came to university applications.

When the four of them exited the bedroom into which they'd just jaunted, therefore, she behaved as if they'd been in there the whole time and offered to make tea and sandwiches.

They all accepted the tea, but, off the back of Stephen's expression, declined the sandwiches.

Now they were crowded around a large, oak dining room table, attempting to make sense both of Carol's experience with Abel and what the others had discovered.

Papers and photos were spread over the tablecloth, arranged into five rough rows.

'I always knew you were a tea leaf,' said Kenny.

Stephen gave him a good-natured shove.

'They're borrowed. Besides, it's all for a good cause.'

'And,' said John, 'we finally have a connection between the missing children.'

'They were all members of the same theatre group,' said Carol.

'And, to one extent or another, all new to the area.'

'Is that relevant?'

'It might be. You said, when you were in Abel's mind, that he had been moved regularly between foster homes.' John held up a mimeographed brochure. 'The *Richardson Community Theatre Programme* is a fairly small group, not particularly well-funded and seems to cater to kids who need an outlet, for whatever reason.' He indicated each of the rows in turn, one for each missing child.

'Mary Haynes. Until recently, her father was in the military, meaning they moved regularly. Andrew Ilett, mother sadly passed away six months ago, he went to live with his aunt and uncle not long after. Lizzie Upton, Katie Robbins and Jane Swannell. All moved to Whitechapel or the surrounding area, for one reason or another, not long before they disappeared. And all joined the theatre group in the last three months, either to make friends or maybe just to get them out from under their parents' feet.'

'What's that about a theatre group?' asked Mrs Jameson, entering the dining room with a fresh pot of tea.

'Nothing, Mum.'

'Don't discount it so quickly, Stephen,' she said, topping up each of their cups. 'Theatre can be a wonderful way to meet some very interesting people.'

Likely not more interesting than members of the next stage in human evolution, Stephen thought, but kept it to himself.

Carol lifted a serviette to her mouth to hide a smile.

Perhaps not entirely to himself.

'Thank you, Mrs Jameson,' said John, on behalf of the group. Stephen's mother gave an approving nod. Of all of his strange new friends, she approved of John most: he had manners.

'Yes, thank you, Mrs Jameson,' the others repeated quickly, appropriately chastened.

'Thanks, Mum,' added Stephen warmly, which seemed to send her on her way satisfied.

'You should all be outside, getting some fresh air' was her parting shot.

'You were saying?' Kenny took a slurp of his tea.

'It's not unreasonable to assume that Abel was a part of the theatre group too,' John continued. 'Perhaps the foster home arranged it.'

Carol furrowed her brow.

'And it would connect Abel to the disappearances, as far as the police were concerned. But why drag him in, instead of any of the others?'

'They can't have known for long,' John said. 'They could simply be working their way down a list and Abel was near the top of it. Abel Brown. It's feasible.'

'No,' said Carol. 'He definitely felt like a serious suspect. I caught an echo of his interrogation when we were linked. They wanted to pin it on him. They thought they had their man. Their boy, anyway.'

'So, there's something else. Something we're not seeing.'

'They would have searched the foster home,' Stephen offered. 'Maybe they found something there.'

'Or maybe,' said Kenny, 'they just thought he was an easy target. Kid with no parents, no one to stand up for him.'

It was a dark thought and cast a pall over the table.

'We need to get TIM back online,' John decided. 'He'll be able to make sense of this far quicker than we can.'

'What if we can't?'

'Don't say that!' protested Stephen. 'Of course we'll be able to.' The thought of losing TIM was

too terrible to contemplate. He might have been a computer, but he was one of them.

'I'm just saying we should be prepared to do this one on our own. In case we have to.'

'What about Ginge and Lefty?'

'I think it would be dangerous to involve them any further.' There was a general ripple of agreement at John's caution. If Abel proved as powerful as he seemed, their sap friends were ill-prepared to take him on.

Just then, Carol, who had been staring at the papers in silence, gave a small yelp.

'What's wrong?'

'Stephen, does your father keep a set of encyclopaedias?'

'Does he ever. He's obsessed with them.'

'Show me.'

Stephen shrugged and led Carol out of the room. When they came back a few minutes later, she held a heavy, leatherbound volume, already open to a specific entry, and wore an expression of both triumph and terror.

She thumped the book onto the table in front of John. He peered at the text.

'The victims of Jack the Ripper,' he read.

'Not this again,' said Kenny. 'I thought you said

this had nothing to do with Jack the Ripper. That it was just a coincidence.'

'I know. But look at the names. Mary Ann Nichols, Annie Chapman, Elizabeth Stride, Catherine Eddowes and Mary Jane Kelly. One, two, three, four, five.'

'So?'

'Stephen, now look at the names of the missing kids. Mary, Andrew, Lizzie, Katie and Jane. It's not exact, but surely it's too close not to mean something. Mary for Mary Anne, Andrew for Annie. Lizzie and Kate, Catherine and Elizabeth. And Jane, for Mary Jane.'

'If the police made the same connection…' John began.

'Still doesn't explain why they leapt on Abel,' said Kenny.

'No, but I suspect it's part of it. We just need to find the missing piece.'

'Are you trying to tell us that Abel is Jack the Ripper?' Stephen was incredulous. 'And we figured it out using my Dad's *encyclopaedias*?'

'No,' said Carol, although a flicker of doubt crossed her face. 'No,' she repeated, more confidently.

'Are we sure?' offered Kenny. 'Whoever or whatever we spoke to… what if it wasn't Abel at all?'

'Who then? Jack the Ripper's ghost?' Stephen shivered. It was an unsettling thought.

'Or something that used to be Jack the Ripper. Taking over people, making them do things.'

John shook his head.

'I don't think that's likely.'

'Why not?'

'Obviously, nothing's certain, but the mind we encountered felt... new. Young. That said, there's clearly some connection. The trouble is...' John leant back in his chair, deep in thought. '... we have two different sets of evidence. On the one hand, we have some idea now what the police have put together. Some link to Jack the Ripper that led them to consider Abel the prime suspect. They'll be thinking that he's playing games with them, at best, and, at worst, that he's some sort of copycat.'

'Let's not assume the children aren't alive and well,' pleaded Carol.

'Oh, I believe they are. Abel's first message told us he needed our help.'

'To stop him doing it *again*.'

'He might have meant the abductions. It was only later than he mentioned killing anyone,' John reminded her. 'The voice changed, if you remember.

Perhaps we were speaking to the Abel we met. To begin with.'

'He didn't remember us.'

'His subconscious? He's in crisis, he might have reached out without even realising it.'

'Fighting back against whatever else is in there with him. Whoever.'

'If Abel *is* a Tomorrow Person, he wouldn't be able to kill. Even if the other voice wanted him to. So, when you made contact, the other voice...'

'We can't keep calling it *the other voice*,' said Carol. 'I'm losing track of who we're talking about.'

'What about Cain?' suggested Stephen, earning a hard stare from the rest of the group.

'Let's go with the second Abel,' said John, 'for now.'

Stephen rolled his eyes. 'You were all thinking it.'

John ignored him and tried to regain his train of thought.

'Where was I? Ah, yes. When you made contact, the *second Abel* must have sensed your power and imagined it had found someone who could help him pluck the fly from his ointment.'

'That's a lot of ifs, mights and musts,' said Kenny.

'It's the only thing that makes sense.'

'Something about this makes *sense*?'

'Kenny, please.'

'Sorry.'

'At this stage, it's what we have.' John was on a roll now, desperately trying to draw all of the connections together. 'Now, the police aren't going to advertise their thinking, not with Abel being a minor and the station already infamous. The newspapers would have a field day. They wanted to have everything wrapped up in a tidy little bow. When Abel didn't crack, or give them anything at all, it must have been a blow.'

'But they don't know what we know,' said Carol.

'About the second Abel...' Stephen was beginning to catch a glimpse of what John was driving at. 'The one who isn't a scared little kid. He has better things to do than turn up for police interviews.'

'Precisely. Which makes the score, for the moment, even. They have one piece of information we don't have and we have one that they don't have.'

'Except there's another thing we don't know.'

'What's that, Kenny?'

'*Why* are there two Abels?'

John fell silent. That was a question he couldn't answer yet.

'One problem at a time. First, we find out why Abel was a suspect. With any luck, that will give us something that might lead us to the missing children. Once they're safe, then we can deal with Abel. Both of them.'

'And TIM, don't forget TIM,' Stephen urged.

'Yes. As much as I think we've proven ourselves capable of doing it on our own, time is running out. If we can get TIM back online, it'll only be for the good.' John clapped his hands together. 'Right, here's what we're going to do. Kenny, you and I will head back to the Lab, get to work on TIM. Carol, you and Stephen, find out why Abel was arrested.'

'I don't think the police are going to be forthcoming,' said Carol.

'Then don't go to the police.'

'Who then?'

John picked up the brochure from earlier.

'I think a trip to the theatre might be in order. Perhaps Mr Richardson can shine a spotlight on the matter.'

Stephen, who had been draining the last of his tea, spluttered dramatically.

'Was that a joke?'

'What do you mean?'

'Never mind.'

The theatre proved to be a poky set of rooms, over two floors, on Whitechapel High Street. Sandwiched between a chippy and a Radio Rentals, it had no signage and only a small paper notice, pinned to the front door – along a large brass knocker bearing the traditional Comedy and Tragedy masks – gave any indication that it had been repurposed as a temple to the Arts.

'If I had to spend my evenings here,' said Stephen warily. 'I'm not sure I wouldn't start kidnapping people.'

'That's not funny, Stephen.'

'It wasn't meant to be.'

Carol lifted the knocker and let it fall. The echo was impressive, but it was followed by a silence that, had it emanated from an end-of-act audience, would have been unbearable.

'Should we try to jaunt inside?'

'I don't want to risk it. Not without TIM online.'

Before they could argue the point any further, they heard footsteps from inside, clearly coming down a flight of stairs. Then the door opened to reveal the harried, cardiganed form of Martin

Richardson, the name given on the piece of paper. Pale-skinned and haggard, he appeared to be in his late forties and wore a pair of battered pince-nez glasses, which sat at a slight angle on his nose; his hair was shoulder-length and tied at the nape of his neck with what Stephen was fairly sure was a handful of elastic bands.

His manner was initially cautious, although his face soon lit up at the sight of two young people on his doorstep.

'Oh, hello,' he said. 'Looking to sign up?'

Clearly, he took them for new recruits.

'Yes,' said Carol, brightly. 'If it's not an inconvenient time.'

Mr Richardson opened the door wide and taking a step back, gestured for them to step inside.

'As the Bard himself says,' he proclaimed happily, '*Better three hours too soon than a minute too late.*'

Catchy, thought Stephen, in Carol's direction.

Philistine, she shot back.

And then, without further ado, the two Tomorrow People went into show business.

John stood up from beneath a control panel and exhaled heavily.

'Try now,' he said.

On the other side of the room, Kenny connected the pair of wires he'd been patiently holding to the corresponding terminals beneath an open hatch.

A very faint hum filled the room, followed by the lights surging back into life. Bio-fluid once more began to move through the overlapping tubes in the centre of the ceiling, the usual shifting patterns of colours resuming their elegant dance.

'TIM? Are you there?'

'I am here, John.'

'Wonderful. We were worried about you. Although, all I could find wrong was a simple short in one of your power units. A self-repair job, under ordinary circumstances.'

'You are quite correct. I powered myself down to prevent further damage from our guest.'

'So, he could have hurt you?'

'He or, more likely, this second voice you described. Which for reasons I cannot yet explain, I am still unable to hear. The young man Abel is quite unlike anyone I have encountered before. Or have a record of in my databanks. And someone of exceptional power.'

'Then he is a Tomorrow Person?'

TIM hesitated. Something that, as a rule, TIM did not do.

'Yes and no.'

John frowned.

'Not a terribly helpful answer.'

'I will try to explain further. Fortunately, before shutting down, I was able to isolate my central processing algorithms in a small, undetectable biofluid unit, which allowed me to continue to work on the problem in your absence.'

'You slept on it,' said Kenny.

'In a manner of speaking, yes.'

'And what conclusions have you reached?'

A holographic image appeared over the link table. A terrifying creature, something like a lion, with a second, goat's, head protruding from its back and a third, this time a snake's, at the end of its tail.

'*That's* Abel?'

'Not exactly, Kenny. I only provide this particular image as a frame of reference.'

'Good, because I do not want to meet that.'

'It's a chimera,' said John. 'From Greek mythology. It also breathes fire.'

'Of course it does.'

'You are correct, John. In mythology, the Chimera is a mythological creature made up of multiple animals, the offspring, in some accounts, of the monsters Echidna and Typhon. Although the term has been used since to describe any creature with parts taken from various animals.'

'And how does this apply to Abel?'

'Chimerism is also the name that Earth science gives to an organism composed of cells with two distinct genotypes.'

'What does *that* mean?' asked Kenny.

'Cells from two different sources, broadly speaking. There are a number of occurrences in nature. During the mating cycle of the Anglerfish, for instance…'

'Forget it. I don't want to know.'

'Perhaps we should skip to the end, TIM.'

'As you wish, John. Chimerism in humans is not yet fully understood, but there have been some significant discoveries. In 1945, for instance, a scientist called Walter Stoeckel first identified something that came to be known as *vanishing twin syndrome*, which meant, in short, that a human child could, theoretically, possess cells from a twin that did not develop, but rather became part of a single child.'

John sat down as TIM continued.

'This might manifest, in its mildest forms, in two differently coloured eyes or shapes of thumb.'

'Or,' said Kenny, 'a lion-goat-snake. That breathes fire.'

'That might be preferable, in this case,' said TIM. 'John, it's possible that Abel is suffering from a much broader split in his internal make-up.'

'You think Abel might actually be two separate people.'

'In ordinary *homo sapiens,* I suspect this would not be possible. But bring into play the evolutionary mutations leading to *homo superior*…'

'Abel is a Tomorrow Person *and* he isn't?'

'Without further testing, we can only conjecture. Abel demonstrated telepathic abilities and seemed to be responding to Carol's help in breaking out. But some part of him also seems willing, even anxious, to kill, which the Prime Barrier should not allow. I hesitate to make a definitive diagnosis, but I would say that his *homo sapiens* and *homo superior* cells are in conflict with each other, which, in concert with the trauma of his powers developing, has had an adverse effect on his mental state. Breaking out is often a time of crisis. For Abel, doubly so.'

John rubbed his eyes. Even with everything he'd

seen and experienced since he'd come into his own powers, this felt like... science fiction.

'Can we help him?'

'I am exploring the possibilities.'

'What about those kids?' asked Kenny.

'In what sense, Kenny?'

'Can he hurt them?'

'At present, I do not believe so. The Prime Barrier is a powerful part of a Tomorrow Person's make-up. What I suggest is that the mental break has funnelled all of his *homo sapiens* aggression into this second personality which, in turn, is now actively working to bypass the new restrictions placed upon it.'

'Can that be done?'

'We are in uncharted territory, John. I cannot answer with any degree of accuracy.'

'Then we have to stop him before we find out.'

'On that we are agreed.'

Mr Richardson led Carol and Stephen down a corridor, towards a small office at the back of the building. The walls, they noted, were lined with framed posters of plays.

'I know it might not look like much,' he said apologetically, 'but we do good work here. I've seen kids your age come through who wouldn't say boo to a goose. A few weeks later and they're rattling off Pinter like it's Enid Blyton.' He paused. 'Don't worry if you don't know who that is yet.' He smiled beatifically. This was clearly his life's work. 'You will soon enough.'

'Are these all the plays you've put on?' asked Stephen, indicating the framed posters.

'Some,' said Richardson. 'Some. But I encourage the children to see as much theatre as they can, in their own time. They often bring posters and programmes back to add to the collection.'

Stephen gave Carol a mental nudge.

'On the opposite wall. Can you see what I see?'

She turned to see what he was looking at.

And there it was.

A tattered handbill in a clean, new frame, dated only a few months earlier, with text that read:

The Half Moon Theatre, 27 Alie Street, London E1.
Ripper! – The Whitechapel Murders of 1888

Episode Four

The second Abel stood outside the front door of a ramshackle, abandoned building and fumbled in his pocket for the key. He was almost visibly vibrating with excitement.

Soon, he thought. Soon, this ludicrous fight would be over and he'd be free of the albatross that nature had hung around his neck.

It was almost obscene how neatly his plans had unfolded. From the moment he'd become aware of himself, a half-thought tucked at the back of another, weaker mind. Filled with rage and the knowledge that he had been done an ignoble injustice.

It had been uphill work, at first, of course. First, he'd tried to make contact with, well, himself, but to no avail. The ungrateful brat either couldn't hear him or was ignoring him intentionally. Probably thought he was a bad dream, or suffering a side

effect of all those headaches he'd been having. Then something miraculous occurred. One night, as the other Abel slept, he awoke, in full control of their joint body. It was minutes, at first, just enough time to look around and get a feel for the place. Then hours, then whole nights. And the longer he spent in the world, the angrier he got about being put away in the morning, like a discarded toy.

It was an intolerable situation, but he soon found a solution. His mind was growing stronger, day by day, fed by the changes happening to their body. He might not, technically, have been the so-called *superior* of the two, but he was developing, even if second-hand, some impressive powers of his own. Before long he discovered that even when confined to his box, he could expand it.

First, he built the *place*. The *place* was his greatest creation and, in many ways, he'd be sad to let it go. But this world was where the real fun was. It was worth the sacrifice.

And then, one night, as his other half sat in the stalls, he was told the *story*. And, oh, what a story. It turned out that there were things you could do with anger and frustration. You could turn them outwards. You could make them *other people's problems*.

Now he was a real boy. Now he had a plan.

He began to pay more attention during the days, as Abel went about his sad, pathetic life.

And made very good use of his nights.

Until he discovered that all that new power came with certain limitations.

He'd sulked a bit after that, he was willing to admit. Which is probably why he didn't notice, until almost too late, that little goody-two shoes, somehow sensing what he'd been up to, had been sending out distress beacons. Without even knowing it.

All of those abilities, in the hands of a milksop. Was that evolution? Was that truly the next stage in mankind's development? To become even more defenceless, even more of a victim?

Still, it all worked out. The Tomorrow People came calling, with a big bag of knowledge in one hand and a potential solution to all of his problems in the other.

And now, he was in control. In daylight, no less.

From the corner of his eye, he took in the street sign that had been screwed into the brick, halfway up the wall.

It was too perfect.

They'll find you.

Abel twitched, his head jerking to one side. There was one new wrinkle he hadn't expected. The little insect had also picked up a trick or two along the way. And he'd barely shut up since he'd had the wheel wrested from him.

'I'm counting on it,' he seethed back.

The key was already in his hand, poised to enter the lock, when he remembered something and laughed.

'I almost forgot. We can travel first-class now.'

Abel vanished in a cloud of light.

'This one sounds a bit gruesome,' said Carol, having drawn Richardson's attention to the framed handbill. 'For kids, I mean.'

The drama teacher lifted his head and peered through his lop-sided lenses.

'Oh yes,' he said. 'A musical, of all things.' He didn't seem to entirely approve of the concept. 'I suppose an argument could be made for *The Threepenny Opera* as an antecedent, but rather morbid for my tastes. And while I'm sure staging it in such close proximity to the actual crimes did

wonders for the box office, it's a cheap trick. In my opinion.'

'So, not from your personal collection.'

'No,' said Richardson. 'One of the students. He was very taken with it, if I recall correctly. But then the young do have an affinity for the macabre. An antidote to the more mundane horrors of growing up, I imagine.'

'Do you remember which student?' Stephen was certain he knew the answer, but there was no fun in solving a mystery and skipping the grand reveal.

Richardson's expression shifted to one of faint suspicion. 'An odd question.'

Stephen shrugged. 'I'm odder than most.'

The teacher gave a sigh of irritation.

'Young man, I enjoy witty repartee as much – more than – the next man, but I think you should tell me why you're really here.'

'Mr Richardson,' said Carol, in a conciliatory tone, 'I feel confident in saying that you wouldn't believe us if we told you. On the other hand, with your vast theatrical experience, I'm equally sure you'd spot insincerity a mile off.' She paused to let the flattery do its work, then nailed the closing line: 'This is a matter of life and death.'

The teacher stared at her appraisingly for a moment, before, in what felt a well-practiced move, steepling his fingers against his chin in thought.

When he spoke, it was with regret.

'I am sorry you won't be joining us. Your delivery was top notch.' Richardson dropped his hands and shoved them decisively into his cardigan pockets. 'And entirely convincing.'

'Thank you, Mr Richardson.'

'The boy's name is Abel Brown, but then you knew that already. You only wanted confirmation.'

'We're sorry for the deception, but it was the only way.'

Richardson nodded, now tense with worry.

'Has something happened to him?'

'We're trying to make sure something doesn't,' Stephen reassured him.

'Then I wish you godspeed. Abel is a charming young man, with great potential. Quiet and, yes, perhaps a little damaged. But I've seen him blossom here. Children like him often do, given a little encouragement.'

Carol smiled softly. Mr Richardson obviously cared deeply about his charges.

'Has he seemed different to you? Recently?'

Having extended his trust once, the teacher now became positively garrulous.

'He's missed a number of rehearsals, but we're inclined to forgiveness here. All of the students have trials enough to face in the outside world. Our aim is to provide a sanctuary, rather than another set of onerous obligations.' He sighed. 'It can be challenging, of course. Most of our productions are staged through pure acts of will.'

'Was Abel often absent?'

'No, as it happens. He's a very dedicated performer, despite his occasional health problems.'

'And you weren't able to check on him?'

'I called the foster home – he's in the care of the state, poor chap – but they were, understandably, circumspect about giving out too much information.' The man's eyes moistened. 'If I'm being truly honest, I've been beside myself. My wife too. She's very fond of the children and of Abel in particular, I think. But we've simply had to hope he would return when he was ready.'

Stephen felt a pang of guilt for some of the uncharitable thoughts he'd entertained about Abel. And grateful that there was at least one person in the boy's life that truly cared about him.

He felt a renewed zeal to pursue a happy ending.

91

'Don't worry, Mr Richardson,' he found himself saying, 'we'll do our best to get him back on stage where he belongs.'

Abel jaunted into the small bedroom, taking great pleasure in the shrieks of the five children and the way they scattered towards the furthest wall. Their clothes were tattered and dirty. Abandoned plates and empty crisp packets littered the floor.

He hadn't ever been able to let them go hungry, not on purpose, thanks to the new quirk in their genetics.

With a growl, he lunged at them, extracting another set of satisfying screams. It was almost worth the white-hot pain that surged through his head, the way it did whenever he so much as tiptoed towards harming them directly.

You can't do it. I won't let you.

'I'm in charge now,' he thought, putting his feeble alter ego in his place. 'And as soon as we've taken care of this little encumbrance you've gifted me, you won't be able to stop me doing anything.'

But why? Why do you want to?

Abel laughed out loud. One of the younger children, Jane, began to whimper piteously.

'Why *not?*'

Mary, Andrew, Lizzie, Katie, Jane.

Abel batted the thought away.

'Stop that.'

Why? Those are their names. It's why you chose them.

'I chose them because they're weak.'

They're weak and you're not?

'I'm only weak because of you.'

And yet I'm the thing holding you back.

'Don't pretend this is nothing to do with you. It was you that gave me the shape to play with. It was you that brought me the *story.* Is it so wrong to want it to have a proper ending?'

I don't want to do this.

'*You* won't have to.' Abel's hatred churned. 'I have other plans for you.' He was being made out to be the villain, simply for acting according to his nature. Like every other product of evolution, he hungered.

Why was it righteous to starve *him*?

Lizzie, the oldest of the children, found a seam of untapped courage and stepped away from the others.

'Just let us go, all right?' she said, unable to keep her voice from trembling. 'You're just a kid, they won't hurt you. They'll get you help.'

Abel roared and lashed out at her, once again knocked back by the pain in his head.

It's never going to work.

Breathing heavily, Abel steadied himself.

'We'll see about that.'

Carol and Stephen appeared on the jaunting pad.

'What did you find out?' John asked, as they stepped down into the Lab. The map of London was once more floating over the table, although Stephen noticed that the only heartbeats it was registering were their own.

'Well, I'm pretty sure we know why the police dragged Abel in,' he said. 'He went to a play about the Ripper case. They must have found something at the foster home. A programme. A ticket stub.'

'Pretty thin evidence,' said Kenny.

'On its own,' admitted Carol. 'But when you take it all together? He would have been on the list of children who attended the theatre group. Then

they discover he's interested in the Ripper case. They make the same connection we did about the names. And, just to top it all off, it's all happening in Whitechapel. Again.'

'And nothing at all to do with the fact that he's a foster kid.'

'I'm not saying you're wrong, Kenny. But neither are they. Abel *is* behind the kidnappings. Just not in the way they think.'

Carol's eyes flicked towards the map.

'No luck in finding him?'

'Abel has apparently found a way to hide himself from us,' said TIM. 'He may have discovered how we were tracking him during his link with you, Carol. Now that he has broken out, at least partially, his powers are only getting stronger.'

'Then we'll have to find another way.'

'We're open to suggestions,' said John.

'It'll have something to do with Jack the Ripper,' said Stephen. 'For whatever reason, the second Abel is obsessed with him.'

'That is understandable,' offered TIM.

'What do you mean?'

'The second Abel is a distillation of all of Abel's *homo sapiens* aggression, gradually splitting off during his evolution into a Tomorrow Person. For it

to manifest fully, however, it would need guidance. It would need context.'

'The play!'

'Yes, John. The play. Abel, entirely unaware of the changes happening inside him, decided to go to the theatre.'

'The theatre was a comfort to him,' said Carol. 'He loved it.'

TIM incorporated this new piece of information into his proposal.

'Making it an even more powerful experience, in that case. But where the first Abel sees a story and is excited by it, the second sees a blueprint. A structure for all of its hostility and violence. It seizes upon patterns, and acts. At first, it only has limited opportunity. Perhaps in the moments when Abel is incapacitated by his headaches. Or when he's asleep. He kidnaps the children, intending to follow the example he's been set.'

'But,' said John, 'he's stopped at the last hurdle by the Prime Barrier.'

'Yes. As Abel grows closer to breaking out, his second self discovers, to its fury, that it cannot kill. It cannot fulfil its destiny. Perhaps, for a short time, it retreats. Attempting to find a solution.'

'Instead,' said Carol, 'it found me.'

'It found us,' John corrected her. 'None of this is your fault.'

'But if I hadn't kept it to myself,' she berated herself, 'if I'd told the rest of you right away…'

'What would we have done differently? There's absolutely no way we could have known.'

'He's right, Carol,' said Stephen. 'There's no one to blame here. Not even Abel.'

Kenny snorted derisively.

'Something to add, Kenny?' asked John.

'He's not entirely innocent, is he?'

'You were just defending him a minute ago!' Stephen threw his arms up in exasperation. 'Saying the police only went after him because he was an easy target.'

'Yes, because they did. You can be right for the wrong reason, you know. But it doesn't change the fact that this second Abel is part of *him*. All that nasty stuff, it came from *him*.'

'That's not fair!' said Carol.

'No,' John held a hand up. 'I understand what Kenny's trying to say. But I think he forgets how lucky we are. To have moved past of all that hate and anger and violence. Plenty of *homo sapiens* manage to do good, to be good, despite all of that still swirling around at the back of their minds. Think about it.

Abel ended up with the worst of both worlds and he *still* tried to stop himself.'

'I suppose so.'

'If we are the next stage in human evolution, we have to do at least that well. Which means we have to step up and do what's best for everyone. Including Abel.'

Kenny cast his eyes down. 'You're right. I'm sorry.'

'There's nothing to be sorry for,' said John kindly. 'I think we've needed to say that all out loud for a while.'

'Okay, so what do we do?' asked Stephen.

'First, we find the children. Then we deal with Abel.'

'Easier said than done, if he's hiding.'

'As you said, Stephen,' TIM explained, 'it is likely that Abel's location, and the location of the missing children, will have some connection to the story upon which he's based all of his actions.'

'That could be anywhere in Whitechapel.'

'On the contrary, Stephen. I have reviewed the facts of the Ripper case and I believe I have already narrowed our search parameters down considerably.'

The map became an image of a single street, abandoned and rowed with dilapidated buildings.

'This is Flower and Dean Street,' said TIM. 'A location directly associated with the terrible events surrounding Jack the Ripper. At least two of the people killed lived on the street and it was considered, at the time, to be one of the most dangerous streets in all of London.'

'Sounds like somewhere the second Abel would love,' replied Stephen.

'But he's just a kid,' protested Kenny. 'How's he going to get a house? And keep five other kids stashed away in it?'

'These houses,' the computer clarified, 'are due, very shortly, for demolition.'

'How are we meant to know which one he's holed up in?' said Stephen, standing in the centre of Flower and Dean Street and turning slowly on his heel. A long, terraced building stretched from one end of the road to the other, fronted by iron railings.

TIM's voice filled his head.

'You'll have to look, Stephen.'

'Thank you,' was the sarcastic reply. 'I was planning to just shout and hope he popped his head out.'

'The original buildings were destroyed in a slum clearance shortly after the murders, so I'm afraid I can't be any more precise.'

'I've tried to reach out telepathically,' said John, 'but it would appear that Abel is unwilling to pick-up.'

'Then, we'll have to do things the old-fashioned way.' Carol marched up to the nearest gate, pushed it open and descended a few short steps towards a less than secure looking door. She knocked loudly.

'Carol!' John scolded her.

'We're running out of time, John.'

'He wants us here, remember. Somehow, we're part of his plan.'

'So, we just wait?'

'Although the authenticity of the letters has never been verified, the lore of Jack of Ripper suggests that he taunted the police,' TIM suggested. 'Perhaps, in that spirit, Abel has left a clue.'

They split up and began to check the dwellings, one by one.

'Here! I've found something.' Stephen had disappeared down a forbidding alleyway that lead to the back of the tenement block and his voice, in their mind, was a mixture of excitement and dread.

They hurried to him.

What he'd discovered was a note, in a sadly childish scrawl, pinned to the back door of a particularly battered looking home.

Dear Boss, it read.

'Can you see what we're seeing, TIM?'

'Yes, John. I can see it. It appears to be referencing one of the letters purported to have been sent to the press in 1888.'

I keep on hearing that the Tomorrow People have caught me, but they won't fix me just yet.

'Creepy,' said Stephen, if only to break the silence.

'It is, isn't it?' said a voice in their minds.

'TIM, Kenny, are you getting that?'

'Unfortunately!' Back in the Lab, Kenny was clutching the back of a chair tightly. He'd argued fiercely that they should have all gone together, but he knew he'd have his part to play very soon, if all went to plan.

'No, John. As before, I do not appear to be able to sense *this* Abel's thoughts.'

'You can't hear anything, TIM?'

'I only have contact with the four of you.'

Abel gave a chuckle. 'One of your friends out of the loop? What a shame. I hope you weren't counting on his help.'

'I was, rather,' John admitted. 'TIM?'

'The red little wagon went up the hill at midnight.'

If Abel had any reaction to the non-sequitur, he wasn't sharing it.

'Again.'

'The horse is in the barn, John. The cabbage is immortal.'

Again, nothing.

'We'll just have to make do without you, TIM,' thought John, trying his best to sound despondent.

'I await your instructions.'

'I thought there was a sense of urgency here,' said Abel. 'Don't you *want* to swoop in and rescue all the poor little children?'

Calm, John told himself. Remain calm.

'They're here, then?'

'Sure! Wouldn't be a party otherwise.'

The door's lock clicked, seemingly under its own power, and swung gently open.

'Come on in.'

'He's just told them to *come in*,' relayed Kenny.

If the pressure was getting to TIM, it didn't show, for which the youngest of the Tomorrow People was grateful. The computer's natural calm had a way of rubbing off on you.

'We are nearing the end, Kenny. I may not be able to hear Abel's thoughts, but neither can he hear mine. Therein lies our advantage.'

'I hope you're right.'

'As I have pointed out on several occasions,' replied the computer, with only a hint of pride, 'this is invariably the case.'

'Well, there's a first time for everything.'

John, Carol and Stephen walked through the doorway and into *everywhere*.

It was an impossibly large space and, though apparently solid enough, clearly did not belong to the normal physical realm. It reminded Stephen of the hyperspace through which they travelled when jaunting, but somehow vaster and emptier. It was, however, not without décor. Surrounding them, two images faded in and out, as though projected

on a giant circular screen. A clenched fist. An opened hand. Clenched, open. Clenched, open. Soundtracked by the heartbeat that had bedevilled them from the start, only now beating a thousand times faster than could possibly be healthy.

It was dizzying. Painful.

'Too fast for you?' asked Abel. His voice was all around them, attacking them from every direction at once.

They slumped to their knees, despite the lack of ground beneath them. Their hands slammed protectively over their ears.

Both sound and images slowed to a stop; there was a final dull thump as the picture settled on the closed fist.

'What is this place?' Stephen asked, blinking rapidly as he tried to clear his head.

'You don't know?' Abel's tone was mocking. 'And I thought you were meant to be advanced beings.' He no longer sounded at all like a 13-year-old boy, or even the spiteful shade of one. In the few months or years he had existed, the second Abel had aged rapidly into jadedness.

'Just tell us,' said Carol, 'and let's get this over with.'

'This is where I live, Carol. My house, stuck

between two states of existence. The closed fist of the *homo sapiens* and the open hand of the Tomorrow People.' He gave his creation an admiring once-over. 'It was a fixer-upper, when I got it. But I've done it up a bit.'

'But it's real? It's a place?'

'It's neither. And both. A little like me.'

'Then let us help you,' said John.

'Oh, I will,' said Abel. 'That's why you're here.'

Suddenly, he appeared physically before them, his face inches from John's.

'Let me show you exactly what I'm dealing with.' He held up his own hand, clenched tight. 'This, I don't mind, but I think we can do better.'

A knife appeared in his grip and before Stephen or Carol could react, he plunged it towards John's chest.

Before it could connect, however, there was a thump and the projection around them shifted to the open hand; Abel screamed with pain and stumbled backwards.

'Do you see? I can't even harm you here!' he shouted, clutching his temple. 'In my own home!'

'It's called the Prime Barrier,' said Carol. 'We can't kill people. Not on purpose.'

'Well, I want it gone.'

'That's not something we can do. Even if we wanted to.' John held his nerve. The knife had seemed terribly real and, however much he believed in the Prime Barrier, it had been no fun testing its limits.

'And we don't want to,' said Stephen.

'*You* don't want to, either,' added Carol. 'Not the real you.'

'This *is* the real me!' Abel shouted. '*Homo sapiens*, through and through. The person I was meant to be, before I was usurped by my mutated other half. Though, I will admit, without his powers I might never even have lived, so I owe him something.'

He clicked his fingers, the heart thumped again, and they were back to the closed fist.

'What do you think? Some flowers? Grapes? A quick death?'

'I still don't understand precisely what you want us to do,' said John.

'I want to be separated.'

'And how are we meant to do that?'

Abel grew excited.

'Ah, you see, when we linked, the five of us, you've no idea how much knowledge poured into me. About the Tomorrow People. About your... about *our* powers. It's been hard work sorting through it

all and I can't pretend I understand everything yet, but there is a way.'

Abel closed his eyes, concentrating fiercely. The image of the closed fist. began to shift into that of the open hand, the heartbeat resumed.

And then, abruptly, everything stopped, the two images layered over one another, the sound looping in on its itself, like a stuck record.

Sweat poured down Abel's face. His scrawny frame twisted with effort.

Taking advantage of the distraction, John sent out an urgent message.

'TIM?'

'Yes, John?'

'Now.'

Kenny ran up onto the jaunting pad and touched his hands to the belt around his waist.

He reappeared in the courtyard behind Flower and Dean Street. There was no sign of the others. Wherever the second Abel had taken them, he had them body and mind. But there wasn't time to worry about that for the present.

He had to try to get the children out.

Kenny stooped briefly to retrieve something from the ground, placing it in the inside pocket of his jacket.

Then he opened the door.

The knife reappeared in Abel's hand, and – with his last remaining strength – he launched himself at John, bellowing with rage.

John dodged out of the way, as Stephen and Carol launched themselves at Abel, trying desperately to slow his progress.

The boy flailed under their attack, stabbing frantically in every direction.

The knife glanced Stephen's arm and he let go with a yelp. Carol gave Abel a shove that sent him sprawling and flew her injured friend's side.

'It's nothing,' he said. 'Just nicked me.'

Abel lay on the floor, locked in a painful rictus, as he tried to keep control over the overlaid images around them, Finally, it became too much and the pictures began to flick back and forth again at top speed, the heartbeat pounding like a drum.

The Tomorrow People cried out at the renewed onslaught, as Abel clambered painfully and unsteadily to his feet.

Gradually, everything slowed back to the single fist.

Panting and crazed, he gestured wildly around him.

'Do you want to talk about *real* evolution?' he demanded. 'I am on the cusp of becoming something entirely new. Forget *homo superior*. I'm *homo dualis*. The best of both worlds.'

'Are you sure you mean the best?' asked Stephen, cradling his wounded arm.

'It's all a matter of perspective.'

'It doesn't matter though, does it?' said John. 'You can't do it. Can't hold the two sides in balance long enough for it to become permanent.'

'No,' said Abel. 'One half of one Tomorrow Person doesn't quite seem to cut it. But I'm thinking four *might* be able to manage it.'

Then he made a show of counting heads.

'Oh, that's a shame. We're one short.'

He clicked his fingers and Kenny appeared, seemingly mid-run. Confused, he skidded to a halt.

'That's better.'

John gave a Kenny a questioning glance and received a shake of the head in reply.

Abel gave a mock sigh and stuck out his bottom lip.

'Didn't manage to get to the kids? That's too bad. Don't worry, I'll check in on them when we're finished here.'

'You're insane,' said Carol.

'Quite probably,' he admitted. 'But then I've been through a lot.'

'We can still find another way.' John took a step forward, closing the distance between them. 'You don't have to be in so much pain.' To his shame, Abel found himself taking a step backwards. Then he snarled and stamped his foot, the adolescent in him swimming to the surface.

'No. Stop doing that. I've told you what you're going to do for me. I don't want any other help.'

'We're not going to let you hurt those children,' Carol insisted.

'You don't have a choice.'

'But we *do*. This is a stalemate. You can't force us to do what you're asking. You're not even offering anything in return. You can't hurt us. The worst you can do is keep us here.'

Abel considered this, ashamed to admit it hadn't even occurred to him before. His darker self might seem older, but he was still inexperienced. He still had blind spots.

Which meant there was hope.

'All right, fine! I'll let the children go. They brought you to me, that will have to be enough.'

'Let them go now.'

Abel seemed on the verge of a full-blown tantrum.

'You're still telling me what to do. This is *my* place. We play by *my* rules.'

'Do as you've promised, and we'll do as you've asked,' said John, in the most infuriatingly paternal tone he had at his disposal.

Abel pointed at Kenny.

'You! Go!'

Kenny vanished.

John, Stephen and Carol looked at each other. They couldn't risk communicating telepathically, but the message was clear nonetheless:

This has to end.

Kenny helped the last of the children from the jaunting pad. It had taken a few trips, but they were all safe now. The others already sat dazed around the Lab table, barely able to take in what they were seeing.

It wasn't surprising. The youngest had been in that house for two months and they'd all been there several weeks at least. They needed food, warmth and their own beds, not to mention being reunited with their parents. But, before any of that, the Tomorrow People had to make sure they were permanently out of danger.

Kenny slipped into a small, side room and checked on the first person he'd brought back from the house. On a small cot lay an unconscious Abel. The *first* Abel, TIM had assured him, though it still felt like a risk having him here with the children.

'Kenny?' TIM's voice appeared in his mind. Clearly, he didn't want to give the children a talking room to contend with on top of everything else. 'Did it work?'

Kenny didn't reply. He couldn't, not while there was a risk that the second Abel was still listening in. Instead, he reached inside his jacket and removed of, all things, a small stone, holding it up for the computer's perusal.

It had been TIM's idea. They'd gambled on Kenny ending up wherever the others had been taken. But until that moment, they weren't sure if it was an entirely mental realm or had a physical component. Whether or not anything other than the Tomorrow People themselves could make the trip.

Now they knew.

'Abel,' he thought, as loudly as he could. 'I'm ready.'

The second Abel had grown ever more erratic by the time Kenny reappeared alongside his friends. Pacing back and forth, muttering to himself and biting at his fingernails.

Kenny smiled. He knew what that meant.

He was nervous. Which might make him sloppy.

Carol had noted it too and she risked a quick message to the others. 'He's not well.'

'Really?' Stephen replied. 'I hadn't noticed.'

Abel's head snapped towards them. If he'd overheard the brief conversation, he didn't comment.

'Time to find out,' John told the others.

That Abel did hear – John had said it out loud.

'Find out what?'

'I just want to understand fully what we're agreeing to here. This place, we're actually *here*, aren't we? It's not just in your mind.'

'I made it,' Abel said petulantly.

'You made it?'

'Yes. I had to have somewhere to go. To get away from *him*. Where I could be myself, not just a voice at the back of his head.'

Carol clicked first.

'This isn't just *like* hyperspace,' she said. 'It *is* a kind of hyperspace. A genuine physical manifestation of the split between you.' Her eyes widened. 'But that's incredible.'

It was also frightening. No other Tomorrow Person had shown evidence of that kind of power. The longer the two Abels co-existed, the more they seemed to be amplifying each other's abilities.

'The other Abel...'

Abel bristled.

'He's not Abel. I am.'

'The other boy then. Does he come here, where you're in control?'

'He has to. There's only room for one of us at a time. Otherwise, there's just the darkness.'

'So where is he now?'

'Back out there. Unconscious. He really is very fragile.'

'Still, while either one of you is here, you have full physical form?'

Abel was growing tired of being interrogated.

'Yes. Not that it does us any good. Can't *do* anything here. Can only *be*.' His face lit up. 'But not for much longer. You'll be here instead, keeping me whole. I don't think you'll have energy to do much else. It's a full-time job.'

'What happens to him when you leave? When you achieve balance?'

'I imagine he'll snap right back here.' He looked at them each in turn. 'Although, I'll doubt he'll be in much shape to lend a hand. And if I'm right, he won't last long.'

He smiled horribly.

'In the end, I still get my five victims. Despite your precious Prime Barrier. Top that, Saucy Jack.'

Unfortunately, Abel had been so busy showing off and so pleased with having thought of everything that he didn't notice that at least one of the Tomorrow People hadn't been thinking of *anything* for several minutes.

'I don't think so,' said Kenny, producing a stun gun from the inside pocket of his jacket and firing.

The image surrounding them faded, leaving them standing in a featureless void.

'Go, Kenny!' shouted Stephen, punching the air.

'Yes, but what do we do with him now?' asked Carol.

John ran to the now unconscious second Abel and picked him up, cradling him surprisingly gently in his arms.

'We see if TIM was right.'

The four Tomorrow People stood, exhausted, in the Lab.

'This is freaky,' said Stephen.

'*This* is the bit you think is freaky?' Kenny replied.

'You know what I mean. There's *two* of them.'

'You have met twins before, haven't you?' Carol teased, though after everything they'd been through with both Abels, it *was* disconcerting to see them sitting opposite each other. Both boys' eyes were closed, as if asleep; sensors had been attached to their temples, transmitting data to TIM's databanks.

'Well?' said John.

'It would seem that they are both healthy, *homo sapiens* boys, of approximately 13 years of age.'

'Saps!' exclaimed Kenny. 'Both of them? How?'

'In addition to Vanishing Twin Syndrome,' the computer explained, 'there is another condition that often affects twins or other multiples. It is known as twin-to-twin transfusion and occurs when an abnormality results in one twin receiving too much blood and the other too little. It can, amongst other things, result in otherwise identical twins of different sizes.'

'How does that apply here?' asked John.

'Strictly speaking, it does not. But I thought it would help you picture what I believe to have occurred. As we initially theorised, Abel, the original Abel, was, in large part, *homo superior*, and had begun the process of developing into a Tomorrow Person. The unchanged *homo sapiens* cells of his potential twin, however, were also part of his make-up. This conflict, at the point of breaking out, caused a mental schism – likely due to *sapiens* brain cells that were simply not equipped to undergo the transformation.

'The development of his powers, however, did not differentiate between the two sets of cells, causing, I believe, further mutation. You'll note that

117

the second Abel, ostensibly the result of the *home sapiens* cells, in fact, became far more powerful than his *homo superior* twin. He was able to create a reality of his own, an ability which, to the best of my knowledge, none of you have yet exhibited.'

'I don't know,' said Stephen. 'Sometimes I think Kenny's in a world of his own.'

'It's the only way I can get any peace and quiet.'

TIM waited for the bickering to die down.

'The source of the power itself still originated with the twin who was breaking out. But it was being siphoned off by the secondary personality, driven by its desire to free itself. And its desire to do harm. The angrier our second Abel became, the more frustrated it became, the more power it used up.

'I first became aware of the transfer of power when I realised that I could receive telepathic signals from the first Abel, but not the second. The sheer amount of power being used interfered with my telepathic circuits. Thankfully, as it turned out, in both directions.'

'But how did you know we would be able to separate them?'

'When Kenny reported that he had visited a physical space and seen a physical second Abel,

while the first lay unconscious in this reality, I knew there was a possibility. Then I considered the fact that his heartbeat accompanied his telepathic signals; he had used it as a part of the template in creating a secondary body to occupy his, shall we say, *inner space*. It must have become entangled with his telepathic abilities. It was only, however, when we determined that physical objects were indeed able to travel to and from the space that I felt confident to act on the assumption.'

'Sending Kenny back with a stun gun.' Stephen patted his friend on the back. 'That was impressive. Especially the way you shielded your thoughts from him.'

'Without taking anything away from Kenny's mental discipline, I was able to aid in that regard also, by aligning his telepathic signal with my own, which Abel could not read.

'In addition, his aggression had been warped by the Ripper story. Whenever he sort to do harm, he did so with the intent to kill. The idea of self-defence short of that might never have occurred to him.'

'You still haven't explained why they're both human now.'

'Energy is finite, John. Even for Tomorrow People. Both Abels have *homo superior* and *homo*

sapiens cells, but, on separation, neither had enough power left, after the enormous expenditure already made, to sustain the transition. Their bodies, in an act of self-preservation, have reverted to *homo sapiens*.'

'So, neither of them are Tomorrow People now?' asked Carol, a little sadly.

'For the moment, no. Perhaps, in future, the process may resume for either, or both, along more usual lines, but it is impossible to tell.'

'And how do we know that neither will decide they still want to have another go at being the next Jack the Ripper?' asked Kenny.

'Without the benefit of the Prime Barrier,' added Stephen.

'They are now fully *homo sapiens*. Their aggression levels will be no higher than any other human being.'

'Not much of a reassurance,' said Carol, hugging her arms tight to her chest.

'And with their permission,' added TIM, 'I have made some slight alterations to their memories. When they awake, they will believe themselves to be brothers. To have always been brothers.'

'Abel and...?' asked Kenny.

Stephen opened his mouth to speak.

'Not Cain,' Carol cautioned.

'I wasn't going to say Cain.'

'Really? What were you going to say?'

'Jack?'

'Absolutely not,' said John.

'Something less mythologically resonant seemed prudent,' said TIM. 'And according to my databanks, Alan appeared to be a suitably innocuous choice.'

'Not Tim?'

'No, Stephen. Not Tim. Although it would have been an admirable choice.'

'We still have the small problem,' John pondered, 'of Abel being the prime suspect in the disappearance of five children.'

'That too has been taken care of.'

'Do I want to know how?'

'I did nothing to the children's memories, if that it is your concern.'

'Then what?'

'During the short time we had together, during Kenny's absence, I took them into my confidence.'

'I'm sorry?'

'I told them the truth.'

Four mouths dropped open in surprise.

'Indeed, they were a most receptive audience. Moved, in one case, to tears for our tragic protagonists.

In return, they exchanged some impressively solemn vows never to repeat a word. I think you'll find, when they come to be questioned, that they never saw the face of the person who abducted them. And will provide some useful contradictory information in terms of height, weight and general demeanour.'

'You trust a bunch of kids to keep their word?' asked Kenny.

'It has become a habit.'

'And the police?' Carol wondered.

'Will shortly receive a packet of new, more concrete, evidence, leading them in a series of ultimately fruitless directions. Eventually, I suspect, it will simply become the newest in a long line of unsolved Whitechapel mysteries.'

'TIM,' said John, after a long moment, 'I am very glad you are on our side.'

'As am I, John.'

All eyes turned to the slumbering twins, Abel and Alan.

'Seems a shame to wake them.' Carol couldn't help but feel sad for the loss of a potential new Tomorrow Person, but as endings went, this wasn't a bad one at all.

'They've new lives to begin,' John reminded her. 'And there's no better time to start than the present.'

'Are you sure this isn't going to be boring?' Ginge asked, as he shuffled across the back row of the small studio theatre, pushing Lefty ahead of him.

'It's a classic, Ginge,' chided Carol. 'You'll enjoy it.'

'I don't know. I get enough of a *Comedy of Errors* hanging around him.' He offered Lefty, who looked bemused by the whole experience, as Exhibit A.

'A bit of culture will be good for you,' said Stephen, from behind John.

'Tell me there's at least a break in the middle.'

'It's called an intermission, you big lug,' weighed in Kenny, bringing up the rear.

'As long as there's crisps, they can call it what they like.'

'I'm just glad,' said John, as they all finally settled into their seats, 'that Mr Richardson didn't ask too many questions about Abel's new *brother* turning up.'

'He was delighted, I heard,' replied Carol, next to him. 'Long-lost siblings? Right up his street.' She took a small bag of sweets from her pocket and passed them to Ginge. 'Besides, it's even better than

that. I hear he and Mrs Richardson are talking about fostering the boys themselves.'

'All's well that ends well?'

Carol laughed.

'Entirely the wrong play.'

Then, as the lights dimmed, the Tomorrow People – and their friends – leant back and waited for the curtain to rise.

You may also enjoy…

You may also enjoy…

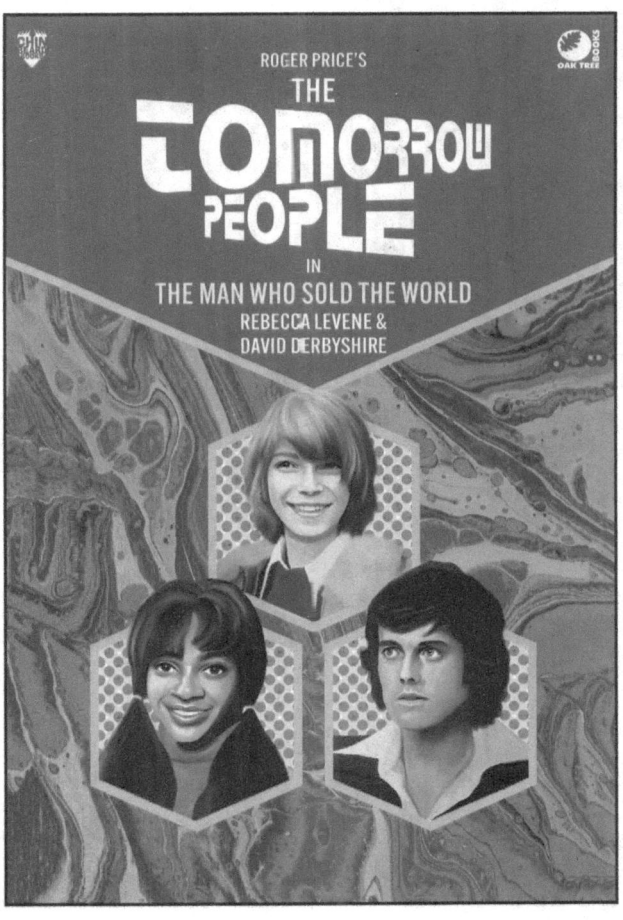

For Scarlet and Hero, who broke out some time ago and are definitely the next stage in human evolution.

Contents

Kenton Hall

The Tomorrow People

in

PRIME FACTORS

A Chinbeard Books / Oak Tree Books Original

The Tomorrow People:
Prime Factors
Written by Kenton Hall
Published in 2025 by
Oak Tree Books
oaktreebooks.uk

in association with
Chinbeard Books

Editor: Paul Simpson
Commissioning/Sub-Editor: Barnaby Eaton-Jones

Cover artwork: Robert Hammond
Layout and Typesetting: Joe Larkins

ROGER PRICE'S

THE

TOMORROW PEOPLE

PRIME FACTORS

Kenton Hall